The Rawhide Years

ADAMS COUNTY
PUBLIC LIBRARY
(COLORADO)
Presented by
THE FRIENDS

1991

© 1987   GAYLORD

Also by Norman A. Fox
in Thorndike Large Print

Reckoning at Rimbow

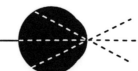

This Large Print Book carries the
Seal of Approval of N.A.V.H.

NORMAN A. FOX

The Rawhide Years

Thorndike Press • Thorndike, Maine

Library of Congress Cataloging in Publication Data:

Fox, Norman A., 1911-1960.
    The rawhide years / Norman A. Fox.
       p. cm.
    ISBN 1-56054-140-7 (alk. paper : lg. print)
    1. Large type books. I. Title.
[PS3511.O968R3   1991]   90-26530
813'.54—dc20   CIP

This book is a work of fiction. Names, characters, places
and incidents are either the product of the author's
imagination or are used fictitiously. Any resemblance to
actual events or locales or persons, living or dead, is
entirely coincidental.

Thorndike Press Large Print edition published in 1991
by arrangement with Richard C. Fox.

Cover design by Ralph Lizotte.

The tree indicium is a trademark of Thorndike Press.

This book is printed on acid-free, high opacity paper.

For
CLARENCE GOLDER,
circus barker and friend

Contents

PART ONE

The Big Muddy, 1879

1

High Stakes

At first, while he went about the evening ritual of swamping out the place, he kept his courage alive by holding to the thought that tonight he would tell Carrico what must be told the man and ask Carrico the question that must be asked. The trick was to think no further than that dread moment. He knew this with a determination that had grown across these last several months, through a springtime of rain and swelling river, through the first hot, oppressive weeks of another St. Louis summer. For him, the time had come. So thinking, he finished with his mop and laid aside his apron, finding in that simple act a high, heady recklessness. But his palms were slippery with sweat, and his breath crowded his throat.

One of the housemen came in by the side door and said, "Evening, Will," and the boy said, "Evening," not really hearing him or seeing him.

It wasn't that he had put aside the one apron that seemed so bold to Will Yeoman but that he hadn't at once donned the other. Each evening he was first a swamper and then a bartender, and the simple matter of trading an apron stained by the dregs of many spittoons for one fresh for the night's trade marked his dubious promotion. The clean apron lay across the bar, and the glasses were arrayed and ready. Very important, those glasses — far more important than the drifting patrons who emptied them of wine and rum and whiskey could guess. Looking at the glasses and remembering the use to which he'd be expected to put them tonight, he shook his head, making his denial, and pulled his hands across his worn trousers to free them of sweat.

Walking across the silence of Carrico's place, with its bar and its gaming tables, its polished lamps and shining mirrors and fine, lush paintings of nudes, he climbed the stairs to his own little room on the landing above. He had passed the clean apron and so broken the pattern of habit. He grew chesty and felt full grown, big enough for anything.

His room was furnished with a makeshift bed and a crude table, and upon that table lay a bundle holding his belongings. A very small bundle. He'd wrapped up a pair of trousers and a couple of shirts, and he'd put in a razor, too, mighty hopeful, for he had only a soft fuzz on his cheeks. The gold coin the man from Montana had given him out of kindness last night was stowed in his shoe, safe from loss. All else lay wrapped in a discarded felt from one of the poker tables, a cloth with a slot cut in it to catch the chips that were anteed each game as a percentage to the house. He hefted the bundle and laid it down again, and Zoe came in soundlessly past the door he'd left ajar.

"Will . . . " she said.

He jumped at her voice and so knew how much of his chestiness had been pure bravado and how tight this last hour had drawn him. But, seeing her, he harked up courage, for she was part of what had turned him bold. She stood smiling at him in her flaring skirt and her low-necked blouse, her black hair tumbled to her shoulders and her red lips pursed. She was olive-skinned and sloe-eyed, full breasted and languid of movement, seeming entirely a woman at sixteen and making him feel always that though he matched her years he was too tall for his britches and too skinny to cast a man's shadow.

He said, "I'm pulling out, Zoe." He nodded toward the bundle.

"Tonight!" Her smiling ceased. "You know

what he expects of you tonight."

"All the more reason," he said.

She moved closer. "Where to, Will? Where?"

He shrugged, making a great show of carelessness. "Downriver, likely. Memphis. Maybe New Orleans. Remember what I told you. I'll write and send you money, soon as I have a job." He looked at her, feeling awkward; he supposed he ought to take her in his arms, and he wanted to kiss her, since this was a good-by of sorts; but he only stood, not knowing what to do with his hands. She was near enough that her perfume crowded at him. He said hurriedly, "It will be real soon. You'll never have to work again, Zoe. I'll take real good care of you."

She held up a hand bare of any rings, and her smile came back with an edge of mockery. "A nigger on every finger?"

"Not at first," he said desperately. "But some day I'll dress you fancy as any lady at the grand balls on Pine Street. Believe me, Zoe."

She put her hands to her hips and tossed back her head. "We'll see," she said. "Have you talked to Carrico?"

"Not yet." A breeze came through the window, lifting the shoddy curtain, a breeze that held not coolness but the piled-up heat of the day. Across distance drifted the whistle of a steamboat and all the muted turbulence of the

14

levee. His skin felt prickly again. "Maybe Carrico doesn't know the answer; maybe the orphanage had nothing to tell him. But somewhere I'll find the way to my name. Once I'm free of here, I'll start searching. I'll have a real name to bring you when we get married."

"Have you told him you're going?"

"I'll tell him tonight."

"He's downstairs now, Will. He came in when I did."

There could be no further waiting, not when waiting only drained him of boldness. "I'll go to him," he said and moved toward the door.

"You're forgetting your bundle," she said making it a jibe, as though she'd said, "You're only bluffing, and you know it and I know it." She had done this to him before, on other nights, needling him when he'd needed bolstering, making him something shameful in his own eyes. He looked at the bundle carelessly to hide his real feelings. "I'll be back for it."

Her mood changed. She came across the room to him, came with a sudden, passionate fierceness and put herself into his arms. Her fingers locked at the nape of his neck and she drew his head down and kissed him, pressing her body tightly against his. Through the skirt and blouse, he could feel her firm con-

15

tours, the straining, demanding body. He got his arms clumsily around her and lost himself in the fire of her nearness; he held her hungrily until Carrico's voice, calling from below, calling his name, penetrated to him and he broke free of Zoe.

"You won't forget?" she whispered hoarsely. "You'll write and send me money? You won't just leave me here?"

"I'll write," he promised and got through the doorway and started down the stairs. But still the feel of her was against him, and still he could hear her voice, like an echo, persisting. She was afraid, too! That was his beating thought. She'd showed him mockery and heedlessness until the last, but that was only so her own fear might stay hidden lest it make his greater. He stayed bold with this knowledge until he saw Carrico leaning against the bar.

Carrico said softly, "Shouldn't the front door be unbarred and the shutters up, Will? We run a business here, you know."

First the planned words came crowding to Will's lips, but before he could say them, he thought, *This last time;* and he crossed to the big front door and swung back the bar and went outside and got the shutters open. He knew he was hedging, and he wasn't proud of himself. He came back inside and walked to-

16

ward Carrico and stood before Carrico.

"Tonight we take him, Will," Carrico said.

"You mean Matt Comfort," Will said.

"Of course. Who else but our expansive storekeeper from far Fort Benton, the man with cattle on the brain. He'll be back, I tell you. He'll be back because for three nights running I've let him win just enough to whet his appetite, and he'll want a last fling before he takes the boat for Montana. Zoe will play her part well enough. See that you do equally well, boy."

He was a fluid man, Carrico; he flowed rather than moved. He was a whiplash of a man dressed in the best of black broadcloth, darkskinned, and with an inky mustache and eyes soft as a spaniel's when he willed them so. French and Spanish and American and German, and perhaps Negro and Indian, too, he might have been St. Louis itself, that mixture of many races and many moods, that blend of turbulence and serenity, handsomeness and sin. He had a cigar between his teeth, a thin cheroot, wine soaked, and when he brought a match to it, the planes of his face showed gaunt and high boned.

He said, "Better get that apron on and be ready. Our man from Montana will be ripe for the shearing, I tell you."

Will said, "I won't be here, Carrico. I'm quitting."

17

"So — ?" Carrico said. He contemplated the glowing end of his cigar and his aristocratic face turned sad. "I saw him give you a gold piece. One that I allowed him to win at my table, incidentally. Is your loyalty greater to a benefactor of the moment than to your benefactor of all the years?"

Will said, "I've been meaning to quit for a long time. I'm not staying another night just to cheat a man who was good to me."

Carrico turned the cigar in his fingers, and the lamplight caught in the rings he wore and sent tiny spears of light dancing. The room lay heavily silent in that moment. Carrico spun suddenly, still holding the cigar, his left fist bunched. The blow caught Will flush on the chin and his legs went out from under him. He sat down hard on the flooring, his head aroar and the salt taste of blood on his lips.

"Get up!" Carrico hissed, his face harsh. "Get up and be about your work!"

Will stared up numbly. He was as tall as Carrico but twenty to thirty pounds under Carrico's weight, yet his first flaring thought was to rise and have at Carrico with fist and boot. Once before he'd tried that, two years ago, when he was fourteen. Carrico had manhandled him easily, for that whiplash body of Carrico's was wiry. Afterwards Carrico had given him a taste of the bull whip Carrico kept in his cubbyhole of an office beyond the bar. The memory of the whip was strong in Will, but what really held him was stronger, made of all the years he'd looked upon this man as master. There were eight of those years, building a barrier too high for sudden surmounting.

He knew that now. He saw himself for what he was, a fool boy who'd tried turning into a man by assuming a man's courage, a stripling who'd talked of marrying and running away and so made a silly figure of himself. This knowledge was bitterer than the taste of his blood.

Only the one houseman was here, the one who'd greeted Will earlier. He sat behind his table and made a great business of shuffling and reshuffling a deck of cards. Zoe stood on the stairs, halted there by the sight of what had happened below. She looked remote to Will, her face a blankness; and this was his greatest humiliation, her seeing him. If she had cried out, ordering him to his feet and into the fight, it might have made the difference.

But the only voice was Carrico's. "Get that apron on. Someone's coming along the street. It may be him."

Will gathered his feet under him and got up. It was another of the housemen who entered. Will picked up the apron and got be-

19

hind the bar. Another houseman came in and another. These were the deadfaced ones who wore green eyeshades and presided over the roulette wheels and the faro banks; poker was Carrico's game, and the main table he ran himself.

Carrico moved now to his table and seated himself and began stacking chips. Trade drifted into Carrico's and Will served the trade and avoided Zoe's eyes as she moved about the room. Her job was to carry trays when there were orders for drinks from the tables.

A sickness grew in Will, a sickness made from the knowledge that there'd be no leaving Carrico and no asking him the question, not tonight. A sickness turned worse by remembering that moment on the floor and wishing now, too late, that he'd acted otherwise. The words that might have been said came to him, and the things that might have been done. He could have dived at Carrico's knees and the unexpectedness of the attack might have given him the necessary edge. He could have arisen and closed with Carrico and bent the man across the bar. But when he looked over at Carrico, he knew that these were wild imaginings and another chance would make him, Will, no braver.

Carrico still sat alone, impatience beginning to show on that schooled face, but at last carriage wheels echoed on the limestone paving. Shortly the door opened and Matt Comfort came in.

Carrico smiled. "A good evening to you," he said. "I've been waiting for a man of your skill, Mr. Comfort."

The claim of Carrico's place was that it was small and intimate and kept genteel hours, catering to a trade appreciative of the finer things. In the confines of this room, Matt Comfort looked big as a mountain, for he was a bulky man with heavy shoulders and a ponderous head. Forty-five perhaps, or fifty; as old as Carrico, he looked older. His broadcloth was as expensive as Carrico's, but he wore it with none of Carrico's grace. He was a florid-faced man with a big booming voice and a great joviality to him. He was a man used to space and a large way of living. He said, "Something to wet our whistles first," and sat down heavily across from Carrico.

"Your pleasure," Carrico said, still smiling.

Zoe fetched the ordered drinks — Comfort was a whiskey man and Carrico preferred a New Orleans brand of wine — and before they'd emptied their glasses, a hand had been dealt. Comfort grinned at his cards. Carrico asked politely, "Your business in St. Louis is about finished?"

"Going upriver come daylight," Comfort said. "Aboard the *Cherokee*, if that mountain boat can build up enough steam to turn the paddles. Got my store stock all bought for another season and a crew of roustabouts loading it. Last season behind the counter, I tell you. No more peddling prunes and saddle soap and Oneida salt. It's the cow business for me."

"So you mentioned," Carrico said. "I find it hard to believe there can be a future for cattle in Montana. What of those hard winters?"

"Trouble with you St. Louis people," said Matt Comfort, "is that Montana meant nothing but furs to you for a long while. Then it meant gold. But let me tell you something. Cattle were driven into Montana over forty years ago, and Texas longhorns have been pouring in ever since Nelson Story pointed the way in '66. Hell, man, this is 1879, and we've got a cattle boom going in the Fort Benton area. Man named Stocking went to raising horses and cattle on the Teton River nearly ten years back. Three years ago thousands of cattle were driven onto the Belt, Highwood, and Arrow Creek ranges. More have come since. Mark my word, it's just the beginning."

"Your deal," Carrico said.

Within an hour three others had joined the

game — a planter from downriver, a St. Louis merchant out for an evening's pleasure, a steamboat pilot whose boat, like the *Cherokee*, would not back from the levee till dawn. The stakes had been increased, and the chips were piled high before Carrico and Comfort, for the game was between those two, as Will knew. Now his own real work had begun, the work for which Carrico had trained him these last few years. He had to banish his sour thinking and keep clear-minded and ready, for soon Carrico would be closing in for the kill.

Zoe came from Carrico's table and placed her tray upon the bar and gave Will an order for drinks. She looked at Will; she looked through him. He filled the order, and she moved back to the table. Passing drinks among them, she bent low enough beside each of the players so that the cleft between her breasts showed and her tumbled hair brushed their cheeks. No man would keep his mind on his cards with Zoe so near, and this was what Will intended to take her from, this making a show of herself for Carrico's gain.

She came back to the bar and said, low-voiced, "The planter's holding a full house. Carrico's only got a pair."

Since the game was draw, Will now knew all he needed to know. Busily polishing glasses, he placed each one on the bar as he finished with it. Three whiskey glasses he arrayed in a row, and beside these he placed two wine glasses. Three of a kind and a pair. Carrico glanced toward the bar without seeming to raise his head. Will polished more glasses, then moved all the glasses to the back bar. He had warned Carrico not to bet against a superior hand.

He gave Carrico more warnings in the next hour. By midnight the St. Louis merchant had dropped out of the game, and within another hour the planter and the steamboat pilot, their chips dwindling, cashed in. The game was Carrico's and Comfort's. Smoke had turned the room blue, and the roulette wheels clicked endlessly, and a steady hum of talk went on. Will was surprised to see how many patrons the place had; he'd been intent on Carrico's table. Tiredness rode his shoulders, and he felt his stomach churn with the excitement of a nearing moment. The bar glistened wetly before him; he wiped the bar and heard the booming voice of Comfort.

" . . . Like I was saying, the whole trick in raising cattle is to be sure of your breed. Scrub cows are going to throw scrub calves. Right? The same as scrub people have scrub offspring. You can tell a man by the blood that's behind him, and that holds true for cattle. And when the corner's tight, a man or a steer will show what breed they come from by the way they act. Never saw it fail. Show me a good man, and I'll show you a good pappy and grandpappy."

"Better pick up your cards, Mr. Comfort," Carrico said.

Comfort had a look at the five cards that had been dealt him. His was no poker face, and he showed his elation. "Getting a mite late," he said. "How about bringing this to a grand finish? I'll wager everything on the table on this hand. What do you say?"

Carrico fingered his chin. "I'll have a drink to help me decide." He signaled to Zoe. She came to the table and bent over him and took his order and moved to Comfort.

"Whiskey," Comfort said.

Zoe came back to the bar and excitement showed on her, livening her eyes. "Four of a kind," she whispered and Will knew she meant Comfort's hand. *"He's* only got a flush." That would be Carrico.

She moved away with the tray; she looked back over her shoulder and smiled. That smile chided him for an hour long gone, for his brave talk and his poor showing. And her smile cemented his decision, for he knew now what he was going to do and how he was going about it. The trick, again, was not to think of consequences. The trick was to hold to a renewed courage that came from many things — the derision in Zoe's smile, the feel of a gold piece in his shoe, the memory of all the indignities he had known at Carrico's hands, but most of all the wisdom that Matt Comfort had so recently put into words. *A man or a steer will show what breed they come from by the way they act* . . .

And so Will Yeoman carefully polished glasses and set them upon the bar — five glasses of different sorts, a straight.

Carrico looked, and Carrico's eyes brightened. All of an evening Carrico had lived for this moment. "I think," he said, "I'll accept your wild wager, Mr. Comfort." He laid down his hand, showing five spades. "And I think I'll collect. You were bluffing."

"You think so?" Comfort said, and his laughter boomed as he spread out his hand showing four treys.

Zoe, still lingering by the table, drew in her breath so quickly that it sounded like a sob. Carrico half rose, his eyes wild. He said, "Why, damn it — !" and then he recovered himself and his smile came. He spread his hands wide apart. "It's yours," he said.

"Then you can cash in these chips for me," Comfort said. "A good ending to a good trip. You come up to Montana sometime and we'll play poker again. Cattle-ranch style."

"Yes," Carrico said slowly. "This is not finished business," but he was looking across the room at Will as he spoke, and anger had turned his eyes black in the lamplight.

2

Escape

A last patron tarried at the bar. He was a man of great thirst and many reminiscences, most of them having to do with women; but Will Yeoman heard him as a blur of sound, conscious only that Carrico still sat at his table and Carrico still looked at him with that hard sheen to his eyes. Carrico was waiting, and the only bulwark between Will and Carrico's wrath was this one persistent patron. The rest of the trade had dwindled away; the housemen had hung up their green eyeshades and shrugged into their street coats and departed; Zoe had long since left for the little hovel along the river where she lived with her people. Outside, the night had turned silent, with only an occasional carriage rumbling distantly.

At last Carrico arose and moved from lamp to lamp, extinguishing all but one. This was a task that on other nights fell to Will. Carrico came toward the bar and tapped the drinker on the shoulder and said, "We close now." Will felt his stomach tighten.

"Sure," the patron said. He downed his drink and drew his hand across his mouth. He pulled forth a ponderous watch and looked at it owlishly. He was a little man, part of the night's flotsam; he was nobody. He lurched toward the door and closed it after him; his bootheels echoed on the sidewalk until even the echoes dwindled and were lost.

Carrico said in a soft and remote voice, "Zoe wouldn't have read four of a kind for a straight. It had to be your mistake, Will. Only I don't think it was any mistake."

"No," Will said, "it wasn't."

This was the last thing left to him — this facing up to the truth. His punishment could be no greater, and he had now the satisfaction of seeing Carrico's astonishment. Carrico hadn't expected boldness. But that old sickness was back in Will, and again he was seeing himself for what he was, a sixteen-year-old, tall for his age maybe, but no match yet for this man, as the earlier evening had shown. He had in one high moment summoned the courage to betray Carrico at the card table and cost Carrico a small fortune, but that, too, had been a childish act, for the consequences had been foreseeable. Now he had made his say and the punishment would come, and he must take it as the ox takes the goad; he must go on taking it across all the days ahead, for he had made his try at breaking from Carrico and he had failed.

Carrico's patrician face had stilled itself after the first astonishment. He said in that same soft voice, "You have proved rebellious twice in one evening. The lesson I teach you must be a staying one."

He went around the end of the bar and into his cubby-hole of an office and came out with the bull whip in his hand. He had practiced much with that whip, had Carrico; he had got it from a drunken freighter from upriver in an earlier day when the place hadn't been so particular about its patronage. Seeing the whip, Will felt terror wash over him, and a cry built in his throat, but he held it back. He cringed behind the bar. Carrico shouted, "Come out of there!" and when Will didn't move, Carrico sent the long lash across the bar and drove Will out into the room. He came after Will with the whip singing, and Will felt the fire of it. Anger stormed through him then, making him heedless, and he rushed at Carrico, hoping to get his arms around the man.

Carrico laughed and shoved at Will with his free hand, sending Will lurching back against the bar. Carrico retreated a few paces to give

30

the whip freer play. He was liking this task, as his face plainly showed.

Will didn't hear the unbarred front door open. He only felt the gust of air and heard the booming, angry voice of Matt Comfort, and he saw Comfort looming behind Carrico and putting a big hand on Carrico's shoulder, spinning Carrico about. Comfort's free fist smashed into Carrico's face and dumped the man. Carrico let go his hold on the whip and came up like a cat.

"Watch out!" Will shouted. "He packs a sleeve gun!"

But Comfort had already moved in against Carrico. He was beating Carrico across the room with short, choppy blows, never letting Carrico have a chance to shake out the derringer he carried. A savage joy leaped in Will. Comfort pinned Carrico against the bar and held him there and brought a fist up against Carrico's jaw. Carrico's eyes rolled back and all sense went out of them. He folded down into a heap across the bar rail.

Comfort stood back panting, his face not the jovial one Will had known. It took Comfort a minute before he was able to speak. "Been hanging around for an hour," he gasped. "Dismissed carriage at corner. Walked back." He managed to grin, a man pleased by his own stratagem. "Figured if there was any pay-

31

off for you, it was bound to come at closing time. Hell, I saw through that signaling trick before the evening was half done."

Will stared at the fallen Carrico, then shook his head. "He'll take twice as much out of my hide when he comes around."

Comfort said, "We'll not chance that. You're leaving with me, lad."

"Where to?"

"Out of here, first of all. The rest you'll decide for yourself." Comfort flexed his broad shoulders and rubbed at his knuckles. "Lordy, but I'm getting too old for fighting."

"I've got a bundle," Will said and went up the stairs after it. Zoe was gone, but the upstairs room was full of Zoe. He didn't tarry. And he didn't look back as he followed Comfort out of the place to the darkened street.

"This way," Comfort said and led him toward the river.

They moved swiftly along dingy streets of warehouses; they moved in a silence broken only by the echoing beat of their feet on red brick and limestone that still held the absorbed warmth of the day. They moved always toward the levee, hurrying along narrow canyons between high, red brick buildings. A city of red brick, St. Louis. Once, cutting across from sidewalk to sidewalk, Will stumbled over tracks for the horse-drawn streetcars. Comfort helped him to his feet and said, "Turn here," indicating a corner.

Will wondered at the unerring knowledge of this man from Montana until Comfort said, "Marched along here once with Indiana men, all of us singing *John Brown's Body* and shouldering Belgian muskets that could bust and blind a man when he fired one. Marching to the steamboats and war, we were. Pittsburg Landing, we called the battle, but now it's Shiloh." He sighed. "It was another picture when we came back to St. Louis after that fight. They carried us on stretchers up through the streets to hospitals, the citizens turning out to help pack us. Not enough hospitals in St. Louis for the seven-thousand odd that were wounded. A couple of halls got turned into hospitals that April, you can bet. '62, that was."

Now Will saw lights ahead and they were to the landing where the steamboats lay moored, banking the river front solidly as far as the eye could see. Here were palatial boats for the Mississippi trade, deep-draft sidewheelers whose lights rose tier upon tier from main deck to the cupola-like pilot houses atop the texases. Such gorgeousness made Will blink. And here, too, were mountain boats, those innovations of necessity made for the Missouri River traffic, flat-bottomed and sternwheeled,

33

their short upper decks offering little resistance to the winds that roved the high prairies.

It was toward one of these that Comfort veered; but on the levee he paused, and finding a packing case, seated himself on it. He motioned for Will to do likewise. "Let's rest a bit," Comfort said.

The levee was alive with activity. By lantern light and flare, roustabouts both white and colored worked, wheeling cargo aboard the packets, toting fuel. Steam winches screamed and hoarse voices lifted in bawled orders, and somewhere, distantly, a banjo made metallic music. Will judged the boat closest by to be the *Cherokee*, and peering, he made out the name painted on the pilot house. He squatted down cross-legged on the hard stones of the levee. He found himself jumpy, questing the shadows. He said, "He's not going to forget what you did to him tonight. He'll have your hide for that."

Comfort asked, "Carrico? By the way, what was he to you?"

"Foster father, I guess you'd call him," Will said. "He took me out of the orphanage where the sisters were keeping me. He had a wife then, and a fine house out near Cote Plaquemine. I was eight when he took me from the sisters, and I must have been about ten when his lady died. I remember her kindly. I've heard it whispered by the house-men that Carrico was one of those who lost his fortune during the war. The bank let him keep the house for a long time, I guess, but I remember the auction sale and our moving away. Then he opened the place. Mostly I re-member the place."

Comfort said, "Your own people — the Yeomans — they're dead?"

In the semi-darkness Will colored. What was it this man had said earlier about scrub cattle and scrub people? How was a person to know his own value when he didn't know his breed?

"The *William J. Yeoman* was a steamboat," Will said. "Her boiler exploded while she was racing with another boat near Lexington, Missouri. Before she sank, my folks must have had time to put me in a yawl and set me adrift. I was just a baby then. Downriver folks found the yawl along the bank and me squalling in it. That's how I ended up in the orphanage."

Comfort whistled. "Like Moses in the bul-rushes. So you took the name of the steam-boat."

"It was painted on the yawl," Will said. "There wasn't any other name to take. That much of the story I got from Carrico when I was small. If the sisters knew more and told him, he didn't tell me. Before I left him, I meant to ask about the rest of it — whether there was anything that told who I might really be. A man should have a name that belongs to him."

"A man is what he makes of himself," Comfort said. He stared toward the *Cherokee*. Faint light was beginning to show in the east, across the river on the Illinois shore, and a few passengers were now going aboard. "That girl who works as barmaid?" Comfort asked. "I saw you staring at her like a sick sheep. Who is she?"

"Zoe," Will said. "We're going to be married. She's Louisiana folks."

"She's not for you," Comfort said.

Will didn't like the way he said it, so final, so shutting out of Zoe. Words came to him in defense of Zoe, but instead he whispered, "Someone's coming!" for a shape had loomed up out of the darkness.

Will's first curdling thought was that Carrico, recovered from what Comfort's fist had done, had come seeking them. Then he saw that the man was shorter. He was striding resolutely toward them; he was a stocky man, dressed in black and wearing a plantation-style black hat, and his face looked blank. It was a face a thousand years old, a carved face

36

from an old church, a face that had looked at too much of life and grown weary. A black mustache, thick and heavy, hid the mouth. This man paused. "So it's you, Matt. Good evening. Or is it good morning? Going aboard soon?"

"Shortly, Sam," Matt Comfort said. "Sam, this is Will Yeoman. Will, meet Sam Little-john."

"I know him," Littlejohn said. "From Carrico's place."

Will couldn't remember the man, but there were so many faces. All the years had been a parade of faces — faces turned slack or belligerent or jolly by liquor, faces turned drawn or triumphant or dazed by the poker table or the roulette wheel or the faro bank. Still, this was a man who should have stuck in memory. Will said, "I don't recollect you."

"I didn't mean for you to," Littlejohn said. He fished in a vest pocket and drew forth a cigar; he fished further for a match, and that movement swung back his coat lapel. Will caught a brief sheen of light on the shield-shaped badge of a United States marshal. Littlejohn lighted the cigar, his eyes looking over the match at Comfort. "I'll be seeing you when we're aboard, Matt."

"You'll be seeing the boy, too," Comfort said. "He's coming with me."

Littlejohn waved the life out of the match. He seemed to turn more remote; he became somebody up in the sky making a pronouncement. He said, "I think you'll regret that decision, Matt." He strode on toward the boat.

Will said, "He doesn't like me. Why is that?"

Comfort shook his head. After a while he said, "Each day we live adds up to what makes us what we are. The tally turns out one way for some, another way for others. Sam Littlejohn has ridden a rough trail. It has soured him and made him suspicious and secretive. You saw his badge, so you know the nature of his work. But remember this, boy; he's my friend, and some day he'll be yours. And you will never have a better friend."

Will said skeptically, "I'll have to take your word for that."

"Come on," Comfort said and eased himself off the packing case. "We might as well go aboard, too. You can sleep in my cabin tonight, but I'll have to find the captain and see about your passage."

Will looked at the bundle at his feet. "You got me free of Carrico's. I'll always be owing you for that. I'll make it from here alone."

Comfort grinned. "Don't want to be beholden? Is that it?"

Will said, "Time I learned to fare for myself. Time I got started."

Comfort shrugged. "Have it your way," he said as though it didn't matter. "What I've got to offer wouldn't be easy. Maybe you wouldn't measure up to it." He took a couple of steps toward the packet.

Will came to his feet. "Just a minute. What is this offer?"

"Work," Comfort said. "Hard, back-busting work. If you listened to the talking I did at Carrico's, you know I'm going cattle ranching. I'll need a crew, and you'd make a starter. I'd put you on a half-broken horse and keep you going from sunup till deep dark. I'd have you out in weather not fit for a dog and on trails a mountain goat would dodge. You'd be too tired at night to tug off your boots. I'd put meat on your bones, but you'd earn every mouthful of grub you'd eat. Maybe it's more than you want to take on."

Will picked up his bundle. There was that money that would have to be sent to Zoe against the hour when they would meet again. What difference did it make where the money came from — Memphis or New Orleans or far Montana?

He said, "I'll take a try at what you have to offer."

Laughter crinkles showed at the corners of Comfort's eyes, but his mouth stayed serious.

"We'd better be seeing the captain about your passage. The fare will have to come out of your wages, mind you."

Will bent over and removed one shoe and shook the gold coin from it. He replaced the shoe and extended the coin to Comfort. "You can put this on the passage."

Comfort began a movement of his hand as though he were going to brush the coin aside; then he reached and took it. The laughter crinkles still showed around his eyes. "Very well," he said. He headed again toward the boat.

Will followed after him. Queer, he thought, how the cards got shuffled. Five nights ago he hadn't known of this Matt Comfort's existence, and now he followed Comfort and so followed his own star. Yet the man striding ahead of him was no stranger. Not after what had happened when Comfort had come back to Carrico's and had at Carrico with a heavy fist. He, Will, had talked with Matt Comfort no longer than the short while they'd spent on the levee, yet he'd answered many questions and so told Comfort more about himself than he'd told any other person, save Zoe.

But now suddenly there was a question Will wanted to ask, and at the edge of the gangplank, with the packet looming big above them, he stopped Comfort.

40

"You said you saw through that signaling trick," Will reminded him.

Comfort grinned. "Mississippi gamblers were working that one in cahoots with the boat bartenders years ago. Some had the code pretty elaborate. They could signal every card, its suit and worth."

"But still you stayed in the game, knowing," Will persisted. "You had a lot of chips, and you were risking all of them on that last play. Why did you take that chance, knowing the game was crooked?"

"To see what *you*'d do," Comfort said.

"Me?"

"I studied those lean chops and those scared eyes of yours four nights running," Comfort said. "I marked you as a lad with spirit who was making some kind of fight with himself. You were as out of place in that den of sin as an old abolitionist at a slave auction. I gave you that gold piece for a reason. I made a bet with myself that you wouldn't crook a man who'd dealt kindly with you."

"But if you'd been wrong — !" Will began, remembering the heaped chips.

"Point is, I was right," Comfort said. "And you see I was gambling for higher stakes than Carrico knew. Come on now; we'd better find my cabin."

"Sure," Will said.

They climbed a companionway to the boiler deck and moved along its shadowy way. Comfort found a cabin door which was placarded with his name; he opened the door and jogged at Will's elbow, urging him inside. Will dimly made out a table and placed his bundle upon it. Comfort groped till he found a lamp. He scratched a match and held it to the wick and stepped back a pace. The light sprang up and filled all the corners, and thus Will had his first glimpse of the wooden cigar-store Indian that stood there scowling at them.

3

Death Comes Aboard

Sunlight on water, and a vast, shining highway twisting endlessly ahead, broad and turbulent and brown . . . The fragrance of flowers sweeping headily off the prairies; the sun sometimes darkened by rising flocks of birds . . . Engines throbbing, paddles chunking, signal bells clanging, whistle echoes beating back from the bluffs . . . Freight crowding the main deck . . . Passengers lining the rails of the boiler and hurricane decks, exclaiming at the wooded shoreline . . . Gamblers and miners and merchants. Indian agents and sallow clerks. Bluff men in buckskin and staid men in broadcloth . . . A little world of wood and iron and humanity set upon the Big Muddy . . . a steamboat called the *Cherokee* . . .

Past Mobile Point the packet had turned

into the swelling tide of the Missouri, riding the late June rise toward its far destination, Fort Benton, head of navigation on the Upper Missouri, over two thousand river miles away. Of an early evening the lights of Kansas City showed on the shore, and soon Leavenworth became a sighted landmark, and three miles farther Fort Leavenworth loomed up. St. Joseph . . . Brownsville . . . Nebraska City . . . Plattsmouth . . . Council Bluffs . . . Omaha . . . Sioux City . . . Yankton. Look long at Yankton: from here another mountain boat, the *Far West*, began its mission of supplying Custer's command in that disastrous campaign of '76 and performed still another service by carrying Reno's wounded in a record run from the Big Horn to Fort Abraham Lincoln . . . The mouth of the Niobrara. Beyond had lain Sioux country and danger in the days before the red man's sun had set with a victory that had held the seeds of his doom at a place called the Little Big Horn . . . Fort Randall . . . The Bijou Hills . . . Fort Thompson . . . Big Bend . . . Medicine Creek . . . Black Hills Landing . . .

These were the places Will Yeoman came to know, and with each mile put behind, Will, first class passenger by virtue of a stranger's generosity, breathed easier. Perhaps this was no dream from which there would be a brutal awakening. Perhaps St. Louis was forever behind him — St. Louis and the kicks and cuffs he'd known. And so he learned to smile.

His days were exciting days; he ranged the boat from the blackness below decks, rancid with the smells of a varied cargo, to the high pilot house perched atop the texas. He watched the tawny bluffs as the Big Muddy cut down out of the frontier; frequently he heard the thunder of bluffs cut away and caving in. He leaned over the rail by the hour, his eyes trying to pierce the vividly green bottom-land willow thickets through which the steamboat wended its way. Sometimes the boiler deck passengers shot at sighted game. Always there was the new adventure of each bend of the river.

Matt Comfort had found no extra cabin available, so the storekeeper had arranged with the captain that Will share Comfort's own. In the evenings, when the boat lay tied up to the bank — "choking a stump," as steamboat lingo had it — they talked, the wooden Indian, so noble of visage and so fierce, staring at them as it clutched a tomahawk in one hand and a sheaf of tobacco leaves in the other. No man in the world but Comfort, Will decided, would have toted such a thing the length of the Missouri.

"That's for Elizabeth," Comfort had explained. "My girl. She's fourteen. When I kissed her good-by in Benton, I said, 'What shall I fetch you back from St. Louis, Libbie? A bolt of calico for a new dress, or some fancy jewelry to decorate yourself?' 'Bring me back a wooden Indian, daddy,' she said, solemn as a treeful of owls. That's Libbie for you. She'd seen one of those things in front of a cigar store when I brought her downriver a couple of years ago. She'd fallen in love with that big chief. So now she's going to have a wooden Indian all her own."

Dragging out his ponderous watch and snapping it open, he'd showed Will a tintype inside the case. A serene, dark-haired woman smiled from the picture; a pigtailed solemn miniature of the mother also gazed back at Will. There was a bridge of freckles across Libbie's nose. Her eyes, Will decided, were direct as a boy's.

"That's the pair of 'em, son," Comfort had said. "They'll mother the stuffings out of you. Just wait till I see their faces when I unload a wooden Injun and a long, lean, yellow-haired drink of water like you!"

Will gazed at the wooden Indian with new interest. "Have any trouble getting him?"

"Had to do some sharp bargaining. Ran into a Montana man in St. Louis and hap-pened to mention in passing that I was looking for a cigar store Indian. Met him at that place where you worked, as a matter of fact. He told me where I might find a big chief."

Thus there were to be two surprises for Comfort's wife and daughter when the *Cherokee* reached river's end. But that day was too distant for Will to begin dwelling on it, though Comfort talked constantly of Montana in their evenings together.

"How much schooling do you have?" he asked Will.

"The sisters at the orphanage taught me reading and writing and figuring. Mrs. Carrico used to read books to me. Afterwards, at the place, I had to know how to keep accounts for Carrico."

"Cattle are my faith, and they'll be my future," Comfort said. "I've got title to a piece of land along the river, and I've got a brand registered — the Diamond C. No more stovepipe hats and fancy duds for Matthew Comfort. It's a brush jacket and a wide hat and jingling spurs from here on out. And the same for you, son. But with your schooling I can work you in the store till we get the ranch going."

Will had heard a lot of talk of Fort Benton among the patrons at Carrico's place, but Comfort painted a broader canvas for him. "It's quite a town, Will. No St. Louis, mind you, but we're coming along. Sixty boats got up there last season — or as far as Cow Island at least, which is the same thing, since they unloaded Benton freight there. We'll probably do even better this season. We've got merchants and freighters and contractors, a drug store, coal dealers, a dairy, a bakery, a saddlery, and pretty near every other kind of business you can think of. There's dressmakers in town and blacksmiths and attorneys and a tobacconist and an auctioneer. We'll be commencing work on a new county court house before the summer's over. It's a town with a wild past that's settling down to a respectable future. If cowboying shouldn't suit your fancy, there's any kind of job waiting you'd care to name."

But Will was not interested in any prospect save that of working for Comfort. Sometimes, when he waited for sleep to come of a silent night, he dwelt on the life that lay ahead, and always Matt Comfort was in that dreaming. He would pay this man back in cash and in loyalty. But only half their journey was behind them, and the days were still too full for the future to be more than a beckoning, promising hand.

Now they were into wilderness, and the boat never wooded but what the mate went ashore first with a rifle held ready, and often

Will and other passengers helped haul the wood aboard. Will came to look forward to the wooding camps, with their stockades and their alert-eyed woodhawks, and he never left the packet without keeping an ear cocked for a raucous warwhoop — and was a little disappointed because he saw only blanketed agency Indians who squatted dispiritedly on the banks. No more fight in them than you'd find in a stump!

He'd read prodigiously from the paper-backed thrillers of Ned Buntline, had Will, and he owned a vivid enough imagination. The redskin's might was broken, it was true, but hadn't Comfort told him how just last April a lieutenant and eighteen men from the military post at Benton had wiped out eight of Sitting Bull's marauding Sioux they'd caught at Martinsdale, on the wrong side of the Canadian line? Friendly Blackfeet up in Montana were begging for ammunition to hunt and to drive off stray Sioux. No telling what might be hiding in the willows here in Dakota, next door to Montana Territory.

Sometimes they met packets that were downriver bound, the boats exchanging blasts of their whistles; sometimes they found a faster packet out of St. Louis crowding their wake. Then there would be a race for an hour or so, and Will remembered the tale he knew of another boat and another race. At Lexington he had thought, *Here! Right here!* and pictured the exploding boiler, the sweeping flames, the panicked people, reliving the disaster with such reality that he half persuaded himself that it was a remembered thing. But the tragedy that had left him nameless crowded less and less into his consciousness with the passing days. He was too immersed in this new life for brooding.

Often the *Cherokee* sailed serenely along a river swelled by mountain snows; sometimes they had to "grasshopper" over sandbars, that queer operation by which the boat lifted itself by its own power. Long, heavy spars, looking like telegraph poles, were raised and set in the river bottom on either side of the boat, their tops inclined toward the bow. Each spar was rigged with a tackle-block, and an end of a long manila cable was fastened to the gunwale and the other end wound around a capstan. As the capstan turned, the packet was lifted and moved forward, the spars then being reset farther ahead and the whole business repeated. Made the boat look like a grasshopper, with those spars jutting up. It was an experience that grew more frequent as the river became shallower than it had been below. Will watched it always with fascinated eyes.

He made friends easily. He penetrated into

the hallowed precincts of the pilot house with impunity; he called the boiler room crew by their first names and came to learn their peculiar lingo and so knew that a "reach" was a straight stretch of water and a "sawyer" was a drifting tree with roots reaching to the river bottom. He spent hours watching for "sleeping sawyers" that did not quite reach to the surface and so formed an unseen hazard that might rip out the bottom of the boat. When the cry went up, "Plant a deadman!" he anticipated the digging of a hole on the bank to bury a log with a line attached to the middle so that the steamboat could tie up where there were no trees.

The dour captain became a confidant of his, and many of the passengers talked to him, and he even wrung an occasional nod from Sam Littlejohn. But he got no warmth out of the man. Littlejohn had worn his badge so long that some of its steel had entered his soul. It was said of him, Will heard, that he had a bulldog's tenacity and a bloodhound's nose. Whatever business was taking him north he kept buttoned tightly against his chest.

Some work in Fort Benton, Will concluded. Possibly in connection with the military. Hardly a river job. In earlier days St. Louis's river commerce had been hampered by pirates at a place called Grand Tower, midway between the mouths of the Missouri and the Ohio, and a governor had decreed that all boats leaving New Orleans for St. Louis should go in company. But those days were long past. True, there had been more recent tales of steamboats looted and burned on the Missouri, but Littlejohn didn't appear to be looking for river-wreckers. He kept mostly to his cabin or drank alone at the bar or paced the deck in the manner of one wiling away the days of a tedious journey. At the same time, he didn't encourage anyone's intimacy, and Will began to see him as a shadow rather than a man, remote and lonely.

But on a night when Will came to the cabin he shared with Comfort, he heard Littlejohn's voice from within, and Comfort's heavier voice, and so knew that the two were visiting. And because he heard his own name mentioned, he stood rooted, listening to the shreds of talk that drifted through a door that stood slightly ajar.

Littlejohn was saying, " . . . Told you in St. Louis, remember, and I'll tell you again. You'll regret having taken that Yeoman boy along."

"Shucks now, Sam, why should I?" That was Comfort speaking. "Will's a good lad."

"Let me remind you of your own argument about breeds of cattle and breeds of men,

52

Matt. I've heard you voice it often enough. Consider this boy and the story he told you about his background. You've no means of knowing whether his people were frontier scum."

"And we've no means of knowing whether they were people of class. The *Yeoman* probably carried all kinds, Sam. The odds are fifty-fifty in his favor."

"Not when you take into account the fact that he grew up in Carrico's place. I know that den — which is why I knew the boy, though he didn't know me. Carrico has always played just within the edge of the law; he's a genteel scoundrel just sharp enough to have kept out of jail. And he's trained the boy in crookedness, by your own admission. Do you think you can wipe away that training overnight?"

"But I've told you the boy bucked Carrico by giving him the wrong signal and throwing the table stakes to me!"

"Yes," Littlejohn said. "He countered Carrico's crookedness by a cheating act of his own, which, when you hold it up to the light, is no less a crooked act for all its courage and the individual good it happened to do you. From your account, I would gather that at that time he was fighting mad at Carrico. Thus he chose to do Carrico in. Another night he'll be of a mood to turn against you."

Comfort laughed. "For what? I spent most of my money in St. Louis, though it's true that I'm carrying what I took from Carrico's table, and it's a healthy sum. But if the lad were going to clout me over the head and make off with that money, he'd have done so while the boat was still near enough to St. Louis that he might have walked back. Sam, you're a sour, suspicious man, and the years are making you more so. Was a time in earlier days when you saw an occasional ray of sunshine."

Littlejohn said, "I wish I were wrong in my judgment, Matt. Maybe I *am* wrong. But I know Carrico's place, and some mighty queer birds flocked there. I'm just telling you to watch yourself."

Comfort said, "All this talk has been the wasting of a fine evening to no gain. Let's turn to something pleasanter, Sam."

Will stumbled away. He groped on up the deck and stood at the prow; his hands gripped the rail till his knuckles showed white, the old sickness in him, the sickness of shame he had known in St. Louis. What chance had he to make something of himself when there were those like Sam Littlejohn who would always remember Carrico's place and what Will Yeoman had been? And how was he to prove himself better than people thought when he couldn't lay claim to a blood heritage? These things beat at him in the darkness, and then anger came, washing over the hurt and the humiliation, and he hated Sam Littlejohn. Some day he would face up to that man and show Littlejohn how mistaken he'd been.

Deep into Dakota now, the boat was making a night run under the blessing of a full moon. True, the packet only sloshed along at half speed, for there was no charting the treacherous channel of the Missouri. A pilot who had found a sandbar on one side of the river coming down from Benton might find the sandbar shifted to the opposite side on his return trip.

Will stood watching the moon walk upon the water, watching with unseeing eyes. He stood for a long time. Sam Littlejohn quit Comfort's cabin and came along the deck, grunting something that might have been a good night as he neared Will. The marshal turned into his own cabin.

Shrugging angrily, Will descended to the main deck and dropped into the boiler room. The crew worked half-heartedly, not needing to poke much fuel to the fire at the slow speed they were maintaining. Will watched them. Here, at other hours, he'd found acceptance, a feeling of belonging, but tonight the magic didn't work. These black-grimed men tossed bantering remarks at him, but he had no heart to respond.

Frontier scum! he kept thinking. Who were those people who had boarded the *William J. Yeoman* and in an hour of disaster managed to place their infant in a small boat and set it adrift? Army folks bound upriver? A gambler and his lady? Some scarlet woman without husband or ring but mother enough when doom struck?

Tired from such futile wondering, he waved a hand at the crew and gave them a wan smile and came groping his way back up to the boiler deck. No light showed under the cabin door, which meant that Comfort had already gone to bed, and Will was glad for that. He didn't want talk with Comfort tonight. The door was unlocked for him, as always, and Will entered and groped for the lamp. In the midst of this careful movement he stumbled over the body that lay heaped upon the floor. His fingers wooden, Will got a match aglow. It was Matt Comfort who lay in his own blood, the handle of a knife protruding from his chest.

This much Will saw by the match's flickering light, this and the fact that the cabin was in wild disorder as though men had battled fiercely here. But the only thing that really struck his consciousness was that Matt Comfort was dead.

4

Night and the Wilderness

Grief was a club that drove Will to his knees. The match winked out, and in the darkness he fumbled at the heaped body, not afraid of the blood, not really aware of the blood. He called Comfort's name wildly, knowing there would be no answer. He pawed at Comfort as though to pull the man back to life by this very desperation. He heard his own voice filling the cabin, and it was a stranger's voice.

Comfort . . . He had worshiped the man with all the affection of a waif who had no kin of his own. Matthew Comfort had taken him from an emptiness of existence and promised him everything. Matthew Comfort had called him son — and died tonight. And out of Will's wild, racking grief came a wild anger that brought him abruptly to his feet. Sam Littlejohn had done this! Littlejohn had been in this cabin no more than an hour before. Yet even as this thought stormed through him, Will knew it was ridiculous. He'd thought of Littlejohn because he hated the marshal, but the body of Matt Comfort was still warm to the touch. That meant that the murderer had been here not long ago. Not more than a few minutes, possibly.

He might still be near! Wrenching open the cabin door, Will peered the length of the boiler deck. Darkness lay there, thick under the overhang, and silence lay there, too, broken only by the slow beat of the paddlewheel; but far up, in the shadows near the prow, Will faintly made out a man — or was it two men? He moved in their direction recklessly. He passed Littlejohn's cabin and remembered fleetingly that Littlejohn was the law, but there was no time to summon the law. Not if hands were to be laid on those prowlers of the night.

He came at a hard run toward the shadowy forms, and, drawing nearer, knew beyond any doubt that he was coming upon the murderer. For there was only one man at the prow — the other form was the wooden Indian that had stood in Matt Comfort's cabin.

In his excitement, Will hadn't noticed that the Indian was gone. But he couldn't mistake that uplifted hand with the tomahawk. And now the shadowy figure was toppling the wooden Indian over the rail, lowering it to the river below by a rope which was swiftly being played out.

For a moment Will only stared, seeing this but not believing it. A wooden cigar-store Indian! Had a murder been committed for a thing like that? Then Will closed the distance and was upon the man. Below, on the Missouri's moon-lighted breast, he caught a glimpse of a shadowy yawl. There were other men down there — men who'd leaned heavily against oars to hold the yawl abreast of the steamboat, men who had retrieved that wooden figure that was somehow so valuable that a man had died tonight. But the yawl was dropping behind as the steamboat sloshed onward; and Will's real concern was with the man in his grip.

That man had meant to go over the side, too, into the yawl. But as Will had come at him, the fellow had waved his arm in frantic signal of warning to his partners below. A cool one — too cool to have shouted. He was a big man, as tall as Will and much heavier, and he'd let out a grunt as Will closed with him. They got their arms wrapped around each other and strained and heaved in the darkness. Anger and hate gave Will a strength beyond his own, but the anger and the hate also

59

robbed him of wisdom. He wasn't a match for this man, any more than he'd been a match for Carrico, but he didn't think to cry for help. Not at first.

He struggled in silent fury, trying to haul the man to the deck. Then, alarmed, he raised his voice. The man got the heel of his hand under Will's chin and his palm over Will's mouth. The fellow twisted his hand, his fingers pressing against Will's nose and gouging at his eyes. A muffled scream of agony broke from Will, and pain turned him desperate. He tried hard to squirm free.

He did manage to get his fingers around the man's wrist and so forced that punishing hand away, but the man instantly gripped at Will's throat. Will felt the fellow's fingers tighten, and though another shout built up in Will, it emerged as no more than a gasp. That strangling hand gripped even tighter. Will fought for air, and a blackness deeper than the night's began to swim before his eyes.

Worse than the pain, worse than the crowding unconsciousness was the feeling of being so utterly alone, so helpless. Up above him was the pilot house, and there a man who might be helping him tended the wheel in complete oblivion to a desperate need so near. Yonder lay the sleeping passengers who might be swarming to his aid. Below, the crew that had tried to banter with him a short while ago worked on, not knowing. He was in these frightful moments terribly alone on this crowded little world that was the packet. He wished frantically that some sleepless one would come strolling the deck. He flailed wildly, trying to beat aside the man's arm, but still the darkness crowded.

The man had got him turned around till Will's back was against the rail. Then the *Cherokee*, moving so stolidly along, shuddered. A sleeping sawyer! The shock hammered upward through the soles of Will's shoes, and with his balance threatened he instinctively ceased trying to haul away that strangling hand and instead threw his arms around the man. And suddenly Will felt himself falling through space, falling toward the river, but he was still clinging to the man.

Will's hold was broken as he hit the water. He went deep and came up kicking hard, a wild horror in him as he tried to put himself away from the steamboat before the suction of the paddlewheel drew him to his death. He'd swallowed a big mouthful of muddy water. Above him the lights of the packet were a blur; they moved past him and he felt the pull of the maelstrom that churned always behind. He went under and came up again, choking and gasping. He could swim, but he had never been called upon to swim against such an undertow. He struggled blindly.

The moon was just settling behind the western bluffs. Soon it was gone and darkness lay upon the river, but Will had marked the nearer shore. The lights of the packet turned smaller with distance, and the hard pull of the paddlewheel was gone. Now Will had only the current to fight. He struck out for land, but the shore seemed to elude him, to become no closer. His arms grew wooden, and his clothes were a dragging weight, and he wished he could kick off his shoes. Twice he let himself down, hoping to touch bottom and so wade in, but there was no bottom. He floundered along and was surprised when his knees grated against sand and gravel. He dragged himself up onto a low bank and clutched at the grass and lay wet and panting.

For a long time he sprawled, numb and chilled and weary, and then he forced himself to his feet and stood peering out across the river. Nothing there to meet the eye, no sign of the fellow with whom he'd struggled. Probably the man's confederates in the yawl had picked him up. He tried to sight the yawl on the river's surface and wished for moonlight. A growing sense of futility upon him, he peered upriver where the riding lights of the *Cherokee* were just vanishing around a bend.

He almost called out after the packet until he realized how useless that would be. Dangerous, too, with that yawl somewhere about.

Willows fringed the bank, and a few stars showed overhead, cold and remote and lonely, and the wind made talk in the trees. Will shivered. Never in his life had he felt so alone. He knew that terror could grow with his mood, and he fought against it. That crack of a twig was a natural sound and not the movement of a bear or a skulking Indian. But he could feel a greatness of country around him, this wilderness that was Dakota; and St. Louis loomed warm in his memory with its familiar brick, its busy streets, its sheltering walls.

He put his mind on Matt Comfort, wanting grief as an antidote for fear; but still the wordless murmur of the river along its bank, and the wordless talk of the wind in the trees found their way to him, and he was scared. The physical drain of the fight with the man and the tussle with the river had left him trembling, and when he first tried to walk, he thought he was going to fall. Resolutely he struck out along the river bank, following in the wake of the vanished packet.

He had only his thoughts for company, and they were dark thoughts. He tried again to fasten his mind on Matt Comfort, who lay dead aboard the *Cherokee;* and he wept then, stumbling along, and was unashamed of his tears.

He thought of that mysterious man with whom he had grappled, that man who'd done murder. He, Will, should have got help before tackling the fellow. He should have stopped at Sam Littlejohn's door or gone after the captain or any roustabout who might have been loitering on one of the lower decks. Or at least he should have armed himself — anything hefty from Comfort's cabin would have been better than his bare hands. There were a dozen things he might have done and hadn't, and he flailed himself for his folly.

No one had seen him go overboard, he judged, for the boat had churned on. Seemed as though that sleeping sawyer hadn't done any real damage to it.

It was hard walking along the river bank. Trees barred his way, and bushes were dark tangles to be stumbled through; and sometimes, when he crowded close to the river, the bank began crumbling under his feet. Mosquitoes were a constant torment, though there was breeze enough to drive most of them away. He batted at mosquitoes ceaselessly and kept moving. The walking warmed him a little. He had no destination, really, but only a hope that he might overtake the steamboat. Now that the last of the moonlight was gone, the *Cherokee* would surely tie up for the night, once the pilot found safe berthing. Will hoped hard that they'd choke a stump on his side of the river.

He wished he knew the country so that he might strike overland, which would mean easier walking and shorter. The way the Missouri twisted and turned, a bottleneck of land only a mile wide sometimes separated two windings of the river that it took a boat a day to cover. On the lower river, passengers wanting to stretch their legs had often disembarked and walked across those narrow stretches, then waited for the boat to overtake them. But the lower Missouri wound through safe country, Will remembered.

Some night-hunting bird beat against a branch overhead, and Will felt the cold needle-prickling of sweat upon his skin. Only an owl, he hastily told himself. He sent his mind ranging for something to fasten upon that would take his fear away, and he thought of Zoe. Queer how little Zoe had crossed his mind of late, but these recent weeks had been so crammed with new sights and sensations that he'd had little time for remembering. He'd aimed to send Zoe money out of his first pay from Matt Comfort, once he'd given Comfort something on the steamboat ticket debt and maybe got himself some proper duds for cow-boying.

Well, there'd be no first pay from big Matt now. He, Will, would be going on to Fort Benton alone and breaking the news to Mrs. Comfort and the little girl with the pigtails. A mighty rough chore that would be! But maybe Mrs. Comfort would still be of a mind to work Matt's land and run cattle under that Diamond C brand Matt had registered. And maybe there'd still be a place on that ranch for Will Yeoman.

So thinking, he tramped onward and at last saw lights ahead. At first he was startled, and then he realized that yonder lay a Dakota settlement. The new Fort Sully, built to replace the one thirty-three miles downriver that had been abandoned in '66? He hardly thought so, recalling talk of the captain's about distances and landmarks just the other day. As he drew nearer, he made the place out to be a small river town, but the thing that really hastened him was the high outline of the twin stacks of the *Cherokee* with the fancy scrollwork between them. The packet had tied up here!

Almost running, Will came into the rude cluster of log and frame buildings and headed toward a makeshift landing where lanterns bobbed. Something stirring there, he judged. He saw a knot of men, black shapes against the shifting light, and he heard the high shrillness of excited voices. He came closer, walk-

66

ing now because there was no wind left in him for running.

Marshal Sam Littlejohn centered the crowd, Will saw when he got to its fringe, and the first words Littlejohn said stopped him, just as that same voice had stopped him aboard the *Cherokee,* outside Comfort's cabin door, earlier tonight. Even as he stood stunned, with Littlejohn's words driving into him, his queer thought was to wonder how so small a man could have so big a voice and put so much command into it.

" . . . Calls himself Yeoman — Will Yeoman," Littlejohn was telling the crowd. "That's the lad. Murdered Matt Comfort in cold blood, from all appearances. Probably for the money Comfort was carrying. The boy was a St. Louis saloon hanger-on Comfort was foolish enough to take under his wing. I warned Comfort that he'd find nothing to trust in the lad. Yeoman went overboard downriver a ways, I'd guess. None of our yawls are missing, and he's the only passenger we can't account for. I'm taking his trail from here. Can somebody provide me with a fast horse? Speak up, one of you!"

In the first moments Will only stood, and then he took a backward step, thankful for the darkness. His first thought had been to step forward and protest his innocence and tell the whole story of what had happened, and much later he was to wonder why he hadn't done so. There was that missing wooden Indian to be explained. Hadn't Littlejohn thought about that? But with the crowd muttering angrily, Will was only remembering that he was a nameless waif who might have done murder, for he could see the situation as it looked to Sam Littlejohn, and he knew how futile it would be to battle against Littlejohn's stubborn conviction of his guilt.

He kept moving away from the crowd until he was into the deep shadow beside a log cabin. From here he could watch the movement down at the landing. The lanterns still bobbed and a murmur of voices drifted to him, but one by one the men moved off.

A pair of them came up from the steamboat carrying a blanket-wrapped burden, and Will knew the nature of that burden. One of these men, a steamboat roustabout, shouted, "Where do we put him?" and out of the darkness the voice of a townsman said, "That carpenter shop over there. It isn't locked. Seth Crosby will knock together a pine box come morning."

The *Cherokee* was staying tied here overnight, Will judged. The people aboard would stay for the funeral likely. Darkness now cloaked the landing, with the last of the lanterns gone and only a dim light or two showing on the packet. Somewhere hoofs beat hard in the night, telling Will that Sam Littlejohn had got a horse and taken the trail. Silence came down upon the little settlement; a door closed nearby; a rooster heralded the coming dawn.

Shortly Will crept away from the cabin and moved to the carpenter shop that had been indicated to the steamboat men. The door gave to his hand, and he groped in the thick darkness until he found the stiffened blanket-wrapped figure that had been laid out upon a work bench.

His fingers told him that the knife had been removed from Matt Comfort's breast. He stood silently by the improvised bier for a long time, no prayer in him, and no tears. He had shed his tears on the river bank; he had wrung himself dry of grief. After a while he groped out of the shop and out of the settlement and stumbled along the river bank again. Soon he veered away and struck overland aimlessly, knowing only that he was heading westward.

He had found a friend and lost him; he had seen a new life open only to have the door closed in his face. There could be no going to Mrs. Comfort now. And there could be no returning to St. Louis, for Littlejohn would have lawmen friends notified to watch for him. He had come up the river with hope; he left the river with bitterness in his heart and a charge of murder dogging his heels and a man hunting him somewhere yonder. Ahead the unborn days stretched, an endlessness of hunger and fear and loneliness. Thus the cards had fallen, and thus they lay as the night and the wilderness swallowed him and he pushed on without destination.

PART TWO

The High Prairie, 1887

5

Stirrup Brothers

Will Yeoman had got his bank and post office business done and bought himself a barber shop shave and haircut and bath as well; and now he sat at the end of the mercantile porch, his legs dangling over, while he waited for Buck Harper. Will frowned. Quite an experience this, having a saddle pard, but not an experience entirely to his liking. He flicked the reins he was holding. Buck made good company, but when a man had ridden long alone and with a shadow on him, the old solitary habits clung hard, especially when there was safety in them. Will had to think about that side of it.

He rolled himself a cigarette and looked along the street. Cottonwoods were getting ready to shed their leaves, and a wind with teeth bit at the dust and hoisted scraps of paper and sent them swirling.

Will's cigarette went out, and he fired it

again; he wasn't too adept at rolling a cigarette, and he didn't suppose he'd ever get so he could do it one-handed. He picked up the reins he'd clamped between his knees while he'd worked with tobacco and paper; he spoke softly to the little bay gelding he'd bought out of Two Cross wages. Buck was certainly taking his time. But all Will had to do was climb aboard the gelding and light out, leaving Buck to ride alone. It could be as simple as that.

Then Buck came out of the store. He had a bundle under one arm — the pair of pants he'd spoken of buying, likely — and he had an open can of tomatoes in his hand. He drained the last of the juice from the can and hurled it out into the wagon-rutted street. He grinned at Will and said, "You look pretty, and you smell pretty. Was there a dance in this town tonight, I'd say let's stay for it."

Will grinned, too. "Bought a Wells Fargo order at the bank and got it into the mail. That cut a hole in last summer's pay bigger than what the barber took."

Buck said, "Anybody who'd mail money to a girl he hasn't seen in eight years is a damn' fool."

Will's grin faded. He didn't mind Buck's opinion; he'd shared tobacco and blankets with Buck many a night, and that gave them the right to talk plain to each other. Trouble was, he'd told Buck about Zoe, not the whole story but enough of it to let Buck know why he'd wanted to stop at this town. Next thing he'd be telling Buck all of it, just to get it off his chest. A secret was safe only when it belonged to one person.

And maybe Buck was right in his notion. Maybe he, Will, *was* a damn' fool to be sending money to Zoe after all these years. Zoe might be married or gone from St. Louis, for all he knew. But he'd kept remembering her whispering, "You'll write and send me money? You won't just leave me here?" until it haunted him, giving him no rest. That money he'd just sent could be the beginning of a stake that would bring her to him some day, if she were still so minded.

"Well," Buck said, "do we drink this town dry, or do we start riding?" He was young, Buck, and lean and full of paint and vinegar. He had a sharp, dark face and a shock of black hair showing under his hat, and all his moods were quick. He gazed about at this Pintoville, this cowtown, this clutter of frame and false-fronts upon the prairie. "That the bank yonder?" He aimed a finger at a clapboard building across the way. "Hell, a man could kick ·in the side with his boot. Will, it's a wonder anybody works when the touches

75

could be so soft."

Will said, "You want to help build that new wall and towers they're talking about putting on the pen at Deer Lodge?" Here was another thing wrong with keeping company with Buck; he got these wayward notions and had to be talked out of them.

Buck shrugged. "Considering what last winter did to the range, there probably wouldn't be enough in that bank to stuff a saddlebag. Trouble with me is that I come from a long line of people who could always hire the work done. Family had a house in Texas with columns in front and black boys walking soft. Or so I'm told. The war wiped them out. Me, I cut my teeth on a horseshoe and sweated from scratch." He stretched himself and came down the steps to the hitchrail where his paint horse stood. "Will, let's head up to Fort Benton. A man-size poker game could roll our summer pay into a winter stake. And there's a girl named Trixie I knew a couple of seasons back. You pine for some frolicking?"

Will stiffened. Here it was again — the danger of riding with another. How could he say that he had walked wide of Fort Benton always and figured to keep on doing so? How could he tell Buck without mentioning Sam Littlejohn? He shook his head. "No hurry, Buck. There's a fellow here I'd like to see — a blacksmith I worked for a few years back."

"Hell!" Buck said, surprised. "You never told me you'd been in this town before. I wondered why you'd ridden a whole day away from Bar B before you did your banking business. We could have taken care of that on the Musselshell."

There's a heap I didn't tell you, Will thought. A lot of it had come back to him while he'd been sitting here waiting for Buck and debating whether he should shake loose from Buck. Things like that season he'd put in at the blacksmith shop in this very town, and things that had happened before and after. A hundred things. Like those first days and nights after he'd left the Missouri. Marshal Sam Littlejohn hadn't cut sign on him, though Will had done a lot of looking over his shoulder. There'd been a time when he'd lived like an animal, hungry and lonely and harried. There were hours when he'd thought dismally of surrendering himself, but the implacability of Littlejohn had been rooted deep in his memory, and the instinct to live had kept him going.

The frontier was changing, and Will Yeoman had witnessed a lot of the change. He had come into Montana overland, crossing an alkali country after he'd worked through the Black Hills, and finally he'd caught his first glimpse of the high lift of shining mountains. He had fallen in with a bunch of freighters on the Montana end of the Bozeman Trail, and they'd given him work and taught him how to handle a bull whip, and he had remembered Carrico.

The next spring, though, he had left the freighters to try his hand at placer mining, wearing his knees raw beside many a mountain stream, a gold pan sloshing in his hands; but luck was not with him. He gained only the security of the silent mountains by this venture, that and the lesson that there was for him no quick and easy way to make a living. He knew Last Chance Gulch and Virginia City and Confederate Gulch during that period, but all were places living in a faded glory. He had come better than a dozen years too late.

It was after the prospecting venture that he'd found himself here in Pintoville in the Judith Basin. Let's see, that had been the fall of '80. He'd got a job as apprentice to a burly man who was as hard as the iron he tempered, but he'd only stayed with Lem Singleton till the next spring. There'd been a lot of abuse with the job, and there'd come a time when the blacksmith had laid a fist on him because a shoeing job wasn't finished soon enough. Will could still see the man towering over him, big and burly and hard-fisted. The blow had felled Will, and he'd lain sprawled beside the anvil, anger growing in him and the thought strong that this was St. Louis all over again, with a new master in place of Carrico. Was he to have run from one Carrico only to find himself with another?

He'd got up and come at the blacksmith and fetched him a good one where it took the wind out of the fellow and doubled him over. A boy had turned into a man with that blow. Maybe that was why he wanted a look at Lem Singleton now, to remember.

He'd gathered his duds and drifted the very day he'd had the set-to, and he'd come again to the Missouri, not the lower river he'd traveled but the Big Muddy that cut through the Montana badlands. It had looked mighty good to him, that brown, serpentine old stream. He went to work at a wooding camp, but only for a week. It was a good enough season — thirty-six boats made Fort Benton that year with freight and passengers — and Will watched each passing packet with a certain wistfulness, remembering the *Cherokee* and his own short-lived period of happiness and security. But on the seventh day a mountain boat put in close to shore, and there leaning on the rail of the boiler deck was Marshal Sam Littlejohn, a cigar clamped between his teeth, his somber face turned toward Will. Damned if that hadn't been a moment to bring the sweat out! The boat made no landing for wood, but Will had drawn his pay and was gone within the hour.

Looking back today, he guessed he'd been jumpier than he needed to be. Whether Littlejohn had actually seen him was one question; whether the marshal would have recognized him was another. The two years since last they'd met had turned Will eighteen and filled him out; but Will was taking no chances. Littlejohn, he remembered, was reputed to have a bulldog's tenacity and a bloodhound's nose. Littlejohn would have taken into account the passage of time and wrought himself a new picture of the boy he sought.

Nothing lost, though, for Will hadn't intended staying at the wooding camp anyway. Not any longer than it took to make a stake and maybe have a little left over to send Zoe. But he hadn't sent her money in those days or even written to her. It hadn't been safe. Sam Littlejohn might be having Zoe watched in St. Louis, and Littlejohn could have traced back a bank draft no matter what name Will used when he bought it.

No, there'd been no future at the wooding camp. The Northern Pacific had reached the eastern border of Montana that summer of '81 and was into Miles City by autumn, and the clang of railroad construction sledges was tolling the death knell of the river trade. Soon the packets would belong to the past, and Will, older and wiser, wanted himself trained for a kind of work that would endure.

That was to be for Zoe's sake, too. Somehow, some day, he would contrive to send for her, but only when he could offer her the things he'd promised in St. Louis. He wanted her mightily; and on a distant range with a new name for himself that he could hide behind, he would have her. That much of an old dream he still cherished; the other half, the hope that he would learn his own true name and perhaps be able to assume it, seemed an impossibility. The trail to that hidden truth had to begin in St. Louis, and St. Louis was a place he must avoid, just as he avoided Fort Benton at the other end of the shining highway Sam Littlejohn rode. Meanwhile, though, a man had to be about making a living.

It was Matt Comfort, two years dead, who'd set Will's feet on the right path, for Comfort had prophesied well and truly when he'd said that cattle were to be the immediate future of Montana. Already the longhorns were on a hundred hills; the graze of Texas had grown thin, and the herds had streamed up from the south, bringing with them the men of the Lone Star, the idiom of the border, and a new day. Cattle had come in from Washington and Oregon and California, too, and dairy stock from Wisconsin and Minnesota. So Will Yeoman had come to a ranch in the Yellowstone Valley, recently cleared of marauding Sioux, and become a cowhand.

A damn' sorry sort of cowhand at first, he recalled. But in due time he'd learned how to tail a calf out of a mudhole and haze a dozen steers out of the river breaks without spilling them all over creation. He'd acquired a horse of his own, and a six-shooter, and the skill to use both. He worked hard and was quick to learn, and the hoorawing he took from a bunkhouse full of Texans soon turned to a quiet respect. He'd kept his name to himself, and no man ever asked him for it. He'd been called the Kid and High-Pockets and Strawtop and numerous other nicknames; and since the ranch had paid off in cash rather than by check, he'd not even been required to have an official listing in the time book.

That first winter at cowboying was a mighty cold one, so cold that rumor had it that Fort Benton folks were talking of putting a boom in the Missouri to stop driftwood and so help solve a fuel shortage. A storm in December tied up stage travel for several days.

But Will was to know a worse winter.

He had drifted from one ranch to another, coming eventually to the Two Cross on the Judith. Let's see, it was just about this time last year when he'd lighted down before the bunkhouse door. The hard winter that had followed had broken Two Cross. Buck Harper, who'd already been with Two Cross a season, had told Will they were in for a cold one when white Arctic owls had appeared on the range that fall.

Buck had come up out of Texas with a trail herd a couple of years before, lost his pay in a Miles City poker game, and stayed on in Montana. Buck knew weather sign; and besides, the Indians had drawn their blankets about them and shaken their heads dolefully, tacit testimony to some awful calamity that still lingered in their racial memory. A freeze, a thaw, and a freeze again, sheathed the range with ice, making it nigh impossible for the longhorns to paw down to forage; and the spring saw the coulees and draws heaped with dead cattle, and the prairies glistening with bones. Hollow-eyed ranchers, ruined beyond redemption, had paid off their crews.

Will and Buck had been among those who'd rolled their soogans, cut out their private saddlers, and taken the trail. Will had swapped his first horse for the bay. Jobs were mighty scarce, he soon found, for again change was having its way with the frontier. Some cattlemen, die-hards of the old breed, still pinned their faith in the longhorn and determined to recoup from nothing. Others, longer of vision, aimed at a new experiment, the raising of blooded stock, fancy stuff that would tally up in quality rather than quantity. A small herd, they argued, could be fed through the winters on sun-cured alfalfa, if the weather ever betrayed them again. Will, remembering Matt Comfort's theories, agreed. But small herds meant small crews, and there was many a ranch where Will and Buck were invited to light down and stretch their legs under the supper table, but where there were no jobs for them when the question was put.

Last summer, when Will had turned twenty-four, they'd landed a place with Bar B, a Musselshell outfit that was backed by Eastern capital and run by an Eastern manager who was long on ledger lore but short on cow-savvy. This spread made periodic reports to its distant backers who decided its procedure, and Will knew it was not the kind of ranch to carry a man through the lean winter months just to have him on hand for the spring. Only a skeleton crew would remain after the fall roundup, and they'd held that roundup a full month early and had only a handful of cows to show for it. With that chore done, Will had waited for the axe to fall.

Well, it had fallen just day before yesterday, and he and Buck had felt its impact. Now they were footloose and fancy free and mighty short of cash. And here was Buck talking about going to Fort Benton. Again Will felt the stirring of uncertainty. A year now he'd known Buck and taken pleasure in Buck's company, but still . . .

And again, Buck asked, "What about Fort Benton? That new Manitoba railroad must be building close by. Maybe they'd give us a job."

Buck said this straight-faced, but Will knew he was funning. Buck wouldn't be interested in any job that took him down off a horse.

Will looked along the street. "Just a minute," he said.

He swung off the mercantile porch and started down the road, leading the bay behind him, the reins slack. Late afternoon sunlight varnished the falsefronts with gold, erasing their ugliness, and a few bonneted shoppers showed on the boardwalks, and a few loafers. That barber had been new to the town, and Will had done no business with the bank six years back, but some of these other faces might be familiar if he looked long enough. No one paid him more than casual heed. He came before the open door of the blacksmith shop and saw Lem Singleton inside. The man loomed as big and brawny as ever, and Will wondered now if it had been a lucky punch he'd thrown to double up this man.

Will said, "Busy?"

Singleton turned away from the forge and put one calloused hand up to shade his eyes. He said gruffly, "What will it be, stranger?"

Will said, "I'm trying to cut sign on a drifting brother of mine. We're near of an age. Anybody passed through here lately that looked like me?"

Singleton peered harder. Six years had made him no less truculent, and his voice held the old harshness. "You look a mite familiar, but I see too many people. I don't know you, and I don't know your brother."

"Much obliged," Will said and turned away.

He knew now why he'd paid this visit, and he knew that he'd learned exactly what he'd hoped to learn. These years had made their difference, filling him out, giving him the shape of a man. The aimless waif had become the drifting cowhand, and here was proof of it and the lifting of a shadow. There had been a choice for him: walk always in fear and uncer-

86

tainty, or walk bravely, knowing that the past had been left far behind. Some day he had to break with constant flight, constant skulking; and Lem Singleton had not remembered him.

Buck waited impatiently at the hitchrail before the mercantile. He said, as Will came up, "Well, it's getting on toward dark. Do we head for Fort Benton?"

"Why not?" Will asked, and stepped up into saddle.

6

Wild Town Waiting

He had expected a sedate but busy town, living with the memories of a wilder past. Gone were the days when Fort Benton had teemed with Mexicans from the south, French *voyageurs* from Canada, and buckskin-clad mountain men who ranged all the beaver streams, hog hairy and sharp eyed and smelling more Indian than white. Will Yeoman had heard it told that a man could walk the full length of Front Street on discarded playing cards in those halcyon days when the old river port really roared. But Matt Comfort, eight years earlier, had talked of staid business houses and the settled professions. Will had thought to ride into a cowtown more pretentious than most and made different, too, by the fact that the steamboats still threaded the Big Muddy to this last port of call. But Will had heard that the once tough and swearing roustabouts had brought in the

Helena, early arrival of that season, with a round of hymns.

What he hadn't expected to find at trail's end was a town ablaze with flags and streamers; even the carriages and phaetons and wagons along Front and Main were bedecked with bunting. Color showed wherever he looked. People thronged the streets, the women dignified in their best gowns and the men self-conscious in derbies and high collars and polished boots. Children darted everywhere. Will whistled his surprise.

Buck Harper, riding stirrup to stirrup beside him, grinned. "They've got up a celebration for us, Will. Sure enough. Now how did they know we were coming?"

Will nodded. He was trying to look every direction at once as they wove through the town, taking in the sights. The double-sized brick building of T. C. Power & Bro. was the biggest structure he'd seen in Montana, and he read the signs of other establishments, too. H. J. Wackerlin, Hardware. The dry goods store of Hirshberg and Nathan. The Bank of Northern Montana. I. G. Baker & Co. The Grand Union Hotel and the Chouteau House and the Pacific Hotel and the Overland. Another bank, the First National. And yonder a sign bearing the name of a recent merchant, but on the side of the building, somewhat weathered, bold, blocky lettering that spelled out Matthew G. Comfort, Merchandise. Odd how such a sight could hark up all the old memories.

Buck's sharp face showed a growing perplexity. "Something big's going on here today. Isn't that band music down the street? Let's rest our saddles and taste some restaurant grub and find out what the shouting's about."

Will had just spied a large streamer spanning the street and read the legend: HAIL TO THE MANITOBA CHIEF. "The railroad!" he shouted in sudden understanding. "Look, Buck. They're celebrating because the railroad's come to Benton. That's the answer."

"You're right," Buck decided. He veered his horse to a hitchrail and dismounted and wrapped the reins around the crosspole. "Jim Hill's pushed his tracks to Fort Benton. Some were saying he'd build to this town; some were betting he wouldn't. You remember the talk last summer."

Will dismounted and tied up his bay and elbowed his way across the walk. Buck beside him, they jangled their spurs into a restaurant. The place was packed, and it took them a while to get a table and a longer time to get waited on.

Talk buzzed about, and from it they got verification of their surmise. Last April construction from Minot to the new city of Great Falls had commenced, Hill's men making a record at track laying with up to eight miles of steel put down in a single day. Will remembered the advertisements he'd seen in newspapers that had come his way — advertisements put out by the Manitoba and headed in big type, THE RECORD BROKEN. Nine thousand workmen and seven thousand horses had toiled to push the railroad toward the sunset, new towns blossoming along the right of way. And now the railroad was here.

"Yes, sir," a man at the next table told Buck, "it were only three days ago, on September 26th, that the tracks crossed the Teton. Every rig in town was packing people to the end of the track, and it took ten deputy sheriffs — ten, mind you! — to keep the liquor hawkers from doing business. By the next day townfolks could hear the locomotive whistle and see black smoke ag'in the sky, and there was the steel gangs — a-sweatin' on government grade no more than two miles away. A few hundred of us busted our britches to go have a look, you bet. Yesterday the end of track reached the depot site at noon, getting in one day ahead of the celebration we'd rigged up. But we're gonna have the celebration anyway. Son, history is being made!"

"You folks sure know how to do things up brown," Buck said.

Will sat back watching Buck. A great hand at drawing people out, Buck; he could give them his smile and have their watch and chain for the asking. He envied Buck his easy way, having always, himself, been wary. He'd studied to make himself like Buck, but today it was a lot easier to just sit and listen. He'd felt strangely moved ever since they'd ridden in. This was Fort Benton. On a long-gone day he had left St. Louis with this river port as his destination. Now, after the years, he had come by his own tortuous, tangled way to the place that had been denied him. Some water had gone under several bridges since he'd started from St. Louis. He'd put on pounds, and he'd come to manhood. And now he was here. It was like no other experience he'd known.

He looked at the food that was placed before him and began eating. He could use a steak after the long ride from Pintoville. Buck ate, too, still keeping up a running conversation with the man at the next table.

"All the bigwigs are here, you say?" Buck was asking.

"Nobody else but James J. Hill, hisself," the man said proudly. "He's wearing his stovepipe hat, and he's got his women folks with him, and directors of the company from St. Paul and New York. About a dozen in all. The general superintendent's here, and the general manager. They come in palace cars by a special train from St. Paul. Jere Sullivan — he's the mayor here — and a bunch of the leading citizens met 'em with carriages and escorted 'em first class to the Grand Union. The infantry band tootled for 'em, and you should have heard the people cheer. Hill and his bunch spent the morning lookin' over the town and shakin' hands. This afternoon there'll be a grand procession formed to march to the depot, and a silver spike will be drove. They'll dig it up afterwards, of course. Tonight there'll be a grand ball. I tell you, we're puttin' on a show!"

"Let's take in the spike driving," Buck said to Will.

By the time they'd finished eating, the procession had already formed and was on its way, and they followed by horseback in its wake, caught up in a surge of belated wagons and buggies with bunting streaming. Will's horse got skittish at the colored cloth and all this excitement and had to be held firmly. Will spoke soft words to the bay from time to time. They passed a Catholic church and scrambled up a prickly pear-studded slope and topped a bluff whence Will looked back to see the town sprawled upon the river bank, with the river serene and the bluffs rising on the far side. Beyond lifted the blue of the Highwoods.

In the opposite direction, Will could see the vanguard of the crowd. To the north the Bear Paws stood against the sky. The September sun was hot as any the summer had known, and Will's shirt clung to him with sweat. He took off his brush jumper and tied it behind his saddle. He eased back his hat and mopped at his brow. He asked Buck, "Now why in the name of sense didn't they build the tracks into town?"

"Some argument with Jim Hill," Buck said. "The way I heard it, the town wanted too much for a depot site, and Hill bucked. So Fort Benton gets a depot just two miles out of town!"

Now they moved downward and across a mile and a half of flat and up another long hill to the railroad terminal. A sea of people flowed restlessly here, and Will judged that every man, woman, and child from Fort Benton must be on the scene. Sitting his saddle, he spoke of this; and a man, overhearing him, said, "A lot of Great Falls folks are here, too. They'll be putting on a celebration up there as soon as the track reaches them." The band, some distance away, blew bravely, and Will made out the black broadcloth of the dignitaries. Someone shouted, "There's Mr. Hill's wife and daughter," and Will craned his neck and saw two ladies, one with a white tam-o'-shanter and the other with a red one, both of them looking stylish and Eastern and somehow aloof and cool even on such an afternoon as this.

And then Will heard the train whistle. It was something disembodied flung across space, a cry out of distance. A child, perched on a wagon seat here on the fringe of the crowd, began jumping up and down in excitement, crying, "I see it! I see it!" The wagon team began to act skittish, and a red-faced rancher on the wagon hauled the girl down and held her close to him, fighting the team with his other hand. Will took up the slack of his own reins. Black smoke showed against the sky, and the locomotive's bell clanged, and the train came chuffing along. The band, bright in uniforms, played louder; a great cheer rose from the people.

After that there was speech-making. A local dignitary made an address of welcome to the railroad heads, and President Hill responded at length. Will couldn't catch all the railroad chief said, but what reached him sounded mighty fancy and there was much applause. Another man — a Judge Tattan, the rancher on the wagon told Will — spoke next, and it was he who suggested that Mrs. Hill drive the silver spike. She stepped forward and complied.

"Would you look at that!" Buck said as the spike, surrounded by bouquets plucked from Benton flower gardens, was sunk home. "The man does the bowing, but he lets his woman do the work."

Will twisted in his saddle to ease cramped muscles. He glanced at the sun and was surprised how much time had passed while the crowd had stood through the afternoon, alternately restive and spellbound. But now this phase of the celebration was over, and the procession was again forming to march back to town. Already some here on the fringe were swinging their vehicles around. Dust lifted as the foresighted ones got an early start.

"Some show," Buck said.

Will didn't hear him. Will's attention had been caught by a blur of movement that was somehow out of tune with all the seething motion of a crowd breaking up — a frantic stirring of dust as a buggy, drawn by a team of matched roans, wheeled wildly away over the brow of the hill. Will looked and felt terror strike through him. The cry, *"Runaway!"* rose and beat at his ears, and several horsemen started at a hard gallop after the buggy. But instinct had given Will his own warning, and he had already reined his mount about and was leaning low over the saddlehorn as he spurred the bay.

He hit the brow of the hill and went over it, and sky and earth turned crazy in his vision. He shut his mind to everything save the need to overtake that buggy careening ahead of him. He didn't want to think what would happen if his horse should somersault, or if he should be thrown off balance and go over the bay's head. He clamped his knees hard against the saddle and came thundering down the slant, the horse's hoofs kicking up a small avalanche of dirt and gravel. He saw the buggy hit a rock and almost overturn, one wheel lifting high. He knew that other riders were behind him and to either side, crowding close.

The buggy hit the flat and started across it, the speed of the runaways unslackened. Will spoke to the bay, and his mount stretched out. Here on comparatively level ground, the horse suddenly stumbled and started to go down. *A gopher hole!* Will thought wildly, but the bay recovered stride and galloped on. Will got abreast of the buggy and had a glimpse of two women, their faces taut as one of them sawed on the reins. Will was thinking now of that second bluff ahead, the one beneath which the town sprawled. There the real danger lay. He inched up beside the team; he drew in as close as he dared, and he jumped.

He wanted to close his eyes as he kicked free of his stirrups and left the saddle, but he forced himself not to do so. He crashed against one of the horses and got an arm around its neck and hung on, groping for a handhold on leather. His feet were dragging ground. He felt his fingers close around a strap, and he tugged hard. He realized he was hollering "Whoa!" into the horse's ear. He wondered how near they were to the drop-off. He felt the pace slacken, and then he had brought the team to a standstill. He stood there, still grasping the bridle; he spoke soothingly to the team which stood trembling.

Men came roaring up, a whirling tornado of men, half a dozen in all. They spilled from saddles and surrounded the buggy and the horses, and one asked intently, "Are you all right, Mrs. Comfort?"

Will found Buck at his side. Buck grinned at him and said, "Let go of that team and sit down somewhere before you fall down, you great big hero you."

A man said, "Here's your horse. I caught

him up for you," and he put the bay's reins into Will's hand. He was a big, handsome man. About forty, Will judged. He had a strong, clean-shaven face with perhaps a little too much jaw. Will said, "Thanks, mister — "

"Millard," the man said. "Brant Millard. That was excellent horsemanship you showed. I think Mrs. Comfort wants to speak to you."

Will turned toward the buggy. The earth felt shaky, and he wasn't sure his legs were going to hold him. He ran his hands over himself, glad that no bones were broken. He'd lost his hat, he discovered. Someone handed it to him. He thanked the person and beat the dust from his hat and put it on, and then, remembering, took it off as he moved to the step of the buggy.

The girl had been the one sawing so frantically on the reins. He saw a pert face and some reddish-brown hair showing under a straw hat, and his thought was that the bridge of freckles across her nose was gone. He wondered if he would have known her, remembering the tintype of a pigtailed girl in Matt Comfort's watch. This was the girl grown up. The woman with her was like the picture had been except that the dark hair was now gray-streaked and the serenity had deserted her. Her face looked worn by many worries, but it was still a handsome face. She smiled at him.

"I think we both owe you our lives, young man," she said. "I'm Hagar Comfort, and this is my daughter, Elizabeth. I would like to know your name."

To Will there was no reality in this moment, no sense, but the question, bringing its clamoring alarm, gave him something to hold to. "The name doesn't matter," he said. "Neither does what I did. I just happened to reach your team ahead of the others."

Brant Millard came to stand at Will's elbow. He said, frowning, "If you'd like, I'll drive you the rest of the way to Diamond C, Libbie."

The girl's lips thinned to a severe line. "I can manage for myself, Brant. I'm not usually so poor a driver, you know. Thanks just the same."

Millard shook his head. "As soon as I collect my men, I'll trail along."

Mrs. Comfort said, "We're only going as far as town. Elizabeth is staying for the ball tonight."

This talk gave Will his chance to fade away. He moved back from the buggy a pace or two, then turned and unobtrusively climbed aboard his horse. Some of those who'd ridden out to stop the runaway had already moved away. Will swung in beside Buck and said,

100

"Let's be going."

Buck stared at him long and intently, his sharp face heavy with thought. "From the looks of you, you need a drink," he said. "In fact, I could use one myself. And there's Trixie to see, too." He jogged his mount. "Come along, Will. We've had a full afternoon. We've seen history made and you've showed yourself to be a bashful hero. Too bashful, I'm thinking. I don't know whether you need your nerves soothed or your sorrows drowned, but the same drink will fix up both. Let's go tie onto it."

7

The Name and the Game

The saloon of Buck's choosing wasn't the biggest one in Benton, yet it looked to Will as though the entire drinking population of the town were jammed into the place. President Hill and his party had taken carriages on to Great Falls that afternoon, not to return until the next evening, but the river port was still celebrating. Men were lined three deep along the bar, and men crowded the poker tables and thronged the floor, their voices a blended, constant buzz, their tobacco smoke lying in thick, blue strands upon the air.

Looking about him, Will thought of Carrico's on its busiest nights. No spur-jangling cowboys in St. Louis, ridden in from outlying ranches, but it was only the garb that was changed. The same cravings were in all men, and thus to Will this place was old and familiar.

He and Buck had had another restaurant meal before they'd come here, and they'd gone to one of the hotels and paid for a room for the night. That had been Buck's idea. "No matter how we throw our money around tonight," he'd said, "we'll have a place to sleep." They'd taken their horses to a livery stable, and here again Buck had insisted they pay in advance, giving the same reason. He was well schooled in his own ritual of recklessness.

And now they were settled down to the night's doings; but Buck, freshly shaved at the hotel and wearing the new pants he'd bought in Pintoville, was having his liquor at one of the poker tables, while Will had worked his way to the bar. Buck had wanted him to sit in at the game, too, but Will had shaken his head. Whereupon Buck had said, "Come to think of it, I've never even seen you play penny-ante in a bunkhouse. Don't you savvy the game?"

"I learned all I wanted to learn about poker years ago," Will said.

Buck had frowned, then shrugged. Fishing a twenty dollar gold piece from his pocket, he'd pressed it into Will's hand. "Keep this for me, kid. If I call you to the table and ask for it, tell me to go to hell. No matter how hard I insist, you still tell me to go to hell.

Once I cash in my chips and ask for my money, you give it to me. When I quit a game, I never go back to it the same night."

Will had dropped the money into his own pocket. "Sure," he said.

Buck wasn't calling him to the table. Buck's only signals were to the sweating bartenders that another round of drinks was wanted. Will didn't even know how Buck was faring with the pasteboards, for Will had his back to the game, and the bar mirror didn't give him any real glimpse of the table. The mirror showed him his own lean face, backed by a shifting surge of men. He studied his face and guessed it would do — nothing to get the girls running in circles, but a pleasant face that looked frankly back at him. The cheekbones were a mite high, but he judged there was no Indian blood, not with that yellow hair and a skin that never fully darkened, as did Buck's, no matter how long the sun beat on him.

He was glad to be shed of Buck for a while; he'd had no moment alone since climbing on his horse out there on the flat after stopping the runaway. He wanted a chance to turn the whole matter over in his mind.

At first it had seemed beyond belief that he should thus have encountered Mrs. Comfort and Libbie, but now that he had time to study on it, maybe it wasn't so strange. Hereabouts their home had been eight years ago; here-abouts it still remained. They had sold the store and moved to that Diamond C acreage, thus fulfilling Matt Comfort's dream. Doubt-less they came often to Fort Benton. The run-away had been a queer fall of the cards, but half a dozen men had started out after that buggy, and only by the merest chance had Will Yeoman been the one to reach it first. If he hadn't met the mother and daughter then, he might have crossed their path in the restau-rant or the hotel lobby or even at the livery stable. True, he might have brushed past them, never knowing.

No, it wasn't so odd that he'd met the Com-forts in Fort Benton, but erasing the strange-ness didn't erase the bitterness that had come to him of that meeting. They'd asked him his name, and he'd withheld it, knowing what he would have seen in their faces, knowing that if he'd spoken he'd now be riding far away and fast, a hard-pressed fugitive again. Damned if he'd liked being nobody to the Comforts. Damned if he'd liked having to turn his back on them.

He drank his whiskey, not really enjoying it but preferring it to beer, which made him sleepy. He ordered again, feeling that he should keep drinking if he wished to hold a place here at the bar. He looked at the array of bottles behind the bar and admired the precision with which the bartenders worked; he listened to the hum of talk around him, picking up snatches of words. These people were really whooping it up! Someone pressed in close beside him, jostling his elbow — a Fort Benton businessman from the cut of his clothes and his soft, unweathered look.

This man bought a drink and said to Will, "Have one with me, friend."

Will started to shake his head, then downed the drink he held and said, "Sure."

"Listen to these blithering fools," the man said with a sour smile. "Celebrating their own funeral, only they don't know it. To hear the talk, you'd think we were going to be twice as important a trading center with both the river and the railroad. Have you seen those advertisements the Benton Transportation Company has been buying in the papers? 'Rail and River!' they scream at you. But this is the finish of the boats, lad. Sure, we've had a big season; the thirty-fifth boat arrived yesterday. But the boats can't compete with railroad freight rates. That locomotive bell we were hearing today was a death knell. What started when the Northern Pacific built into Montana will be finished now that the Manitoba has come to our doorstep. Fort Benton is on its way to being just another cowtown."

Will shook his head and decided that the whiskey was hitting him harder than he'd thought. It was an effort to hold to his companion's thread of talk. Anyway, he was glad the man hadn't identified him as the one who'd stopped the runaway. He didn't want to be marked in Fort Benton.

"Railroad or no," Will said, "there'll still be plenty of trade."

"Bah! Industry is going to be the future, not trade. And Great Falls is going to be the industrial center in this section. Mark my word. It's got the water power, and now it's getting the transportation. Doesn't anybody realize that those tracks they built here are two miles out?" The man paused. "Another drink, lad?"

"I'll buy," Will said.

The whiskey was warming him and loosening him; the whiskey was giving the world a bit of a glow. Who gave a damn what happened to Fort Benton anyway? He crooked a finger at the nearest bartender and got a bottle and poured a drink for himself and the man. Someone came elbowing up alongside him, driving a wedge between Will and his companion, and Will turned, half belligerent. It was Buck. Buck scowled and helped himself from the bottle the bartender had slid Will's way.

Will asked, "Through with poker?"

"Those boys were playing for blood, and they really sharpened their teeth on me," Buck said. "I know when it ain't my night." He gulped his drink; some of it ran down his chin. "I'll take that twenty now, Will. I'm flat as a stepped-on road apple."

Will passed over the coin. Buck slammed it down hard on the bar. "I'll take the bottle," he said and got his change. He nudged Will. "Let's find a table to ourselves. I've got jawing to do."

They had to wait before they could get a table, but at last a couple of restive cowboys vacated one in a corner. Buck slumped down and set bottle and glasses before him. He poured drinks for himself and Will. Will sprawled back in a chair and wished there were room for him to stretch out his long legs. He looked at the milling people. This table set them a little apart from the raucousness.

Buck was talking, but Will listened to him with no real interest. Buck was complaining about the way they played poker hereabouts. Will was thinking that it wasn't a bit strange that he'd met the Comforts, not a bit. A man might meet anybody in Fort Benton. Anybody. This was the end of the river and likewise the jumping-off place to all the Montana frontier. St Louis walked here, and Memphis, and New Orleans. And now, with the railroad's coming, there'd be fat brokers from Chicago and wheat buyers from Minneapolis and dirt-begrimed farmers from Dakota. Fort Benton was next door to all the world.

That man might be here. That one whom he'd battled on the boiler deck of the *Cherokee*, the man who'd taken the plunge into the river with him. Often, across the rough, rawhide years, he had scanned the faces of strangers, but that was only habit, and a fruitless one at that. He hadn't actually seen his adversary that night; he only knew that the fellow had been big, hard to hold. Some day they might meet again, but Will wouldn't even know the man if that day came. And since the fellow wouldn't likely know him either, there'd be no betraying sign on the other's part. They would meet and take their separate trails again, and nothing would come of it.

By how many campfires had he thought about that fight aboard the packet? In how many bunkhouses, with the night wind against the windows, had he tried piecing together how it had all happened? Sam Littlejohn had said in that nameless Dakota settlement that only one passenger had jumped the boat, and his name was Will Yeoman. That meant the unknown one had boarded from the yawl to do murder. But whence had he come and where had he gone? And for what purpose?

"Buck," he heard himself ask thickly, "why in hell would anybody steal a cigar store Indian?"

That was the whiskey talking, he knew. Buck stared at him, slack-jawed. Will, himself, was just as startled, and he waved a hand, dismissing the question. He'd have to watch himself! But the whiskey was a good thing, just the same, so long as he held onto his tongue. He guessed he'd pour himself another drink, and he groped for the bottle. He'd done his share of drinking on town nights with the crews of the various ranches for which he'd worked. He'd whooped it up with the best of them, but it hadn't been tonight's kind of drinking, this drowning of something that galled him. Now what was it he was trying to wash under? Oh, yes, that matter of Mrs. Comfort's asking his name and his not being able to speak out.

Buck said, "I've got a deal to talk over." He said this so intently as to swing Will's gaze to him, and Will guessed this was why Buck had fetched him to the table.

"We're running low on money," Buck said. "And jobs aren't dangling from clothes lines. It's time we made us a stake, and fast."

Will wanted to laugh. Ol' Buck was serious

as a treeful of owls. "A treeful of owls"? Now where had he run across that expression? He shook his head. "You thinking about kicking in the side of a bank, Buck?"

Buck leaned toward him, his sharp face screwed tight and a shock of black hair lying sweat-plastered on his forehead. "Not that, kid. I've got it worked out. A bank is what anybody would hit at, or that stage that comes to and from Billings daily. That's why banks and stagecoaches are always primed for trouble. But there's a little store down the street that I got a glimpse of today. It's small, and it won't be packed with customers. Tomorrow we walk in just before closing time and stick a gun in the proprietor's face. We won't pick up the kind of change we'd get out of a bank. But we'll be hitting where nobody will expect trouble, and we'll be ten miles away before they've got over being surprised."

Will shook his head. "Not for me."

Buck looked quickly around to make sure no one was overhearing them. "I'll do the real work," he said. "You go in first and pretend you're doing some shopping. When the customers are either all gone or thinned out, you give me a high sign. I'll walk in with the gun. All you'll have to do is stand by ready in case anything goes wrong. It'll be easy."

Will said, "You're a damn' fool, Buck."

"Look," Buck said and his face had taken on a hard cast. "You're on the dodge already. You've got the name, so you might as well have the game."

Something struck through Will's drunkenness, turning him alert, scaring him. His driving thought was that he must not make any sign to show how hard Buck's words had hit him. He laughed. The laughter sounded forced. He waited till he could be sure of his voice. He said, "You're crazy, Buck."

Buck laughed, too, but it wasn't a good sound. "Am I, Will? Let's see. I've known you now at least a year, but I don't really know much about you, and you've never even told me your last name. You've been tight-mouthed, pard. When we rolled our soogans at Bar B, you had money you wanted to send some gal in St. Louis, but we had to put a day's riding behind us before you found a post office far enough away from the Musselshell for your liking. You weren't busting with eagerness to come to Fort Benton, either. And today, when that lady asked you your name, you faded out fast. Warming up to her might have meant a winter's job for both of us, or at least a place to roundside for a few days with three squares set out on the table. But all you wanted to do was duck. It all adds up. You're on the dodge, Will."

Will didn't speak. Here, then, was the very thing he'd feared when he'd debated with himself in Pintoville as to whether he should ride out alone, shaking Buck. Here was what came of having a saddle pard, this standing naked when he'd thought himself protected. He'd ridden one mile too many with Buck. Then he felt the pressure of Buck's fingers on his arm, and he looked up to find Buck grinning at him.

"Hell, it's safe with me," Buck said. "Maybe whatever is worrying you makes a good reason in your mind why you shouldn't pull anything shady in Benton, like the store job. I ain't asking, kid."

Will said, "We'll see. I've got to think about it." *The name and the game.* But he still felt that he didn't want any part of this business of throwing a gun into the teeth of some store owner. He wanted to swing Buck's mind away from such a notion. He said, "I thought you aimed to see some girl named Trixie."

Buck's grin broadened. "Don't think she hasn't been on the edge of my mind all along. There were four girls at her place, last time I dropped in. You come, too, Will. We might as well be flat busted as the way we are."

Will shook his head. "I've never taken my fun that way."

113

"Time you did," Buck said. "A man's got to wake up to the fact that he's a man sooner or later. Come on, Will." He poured them each another drink, then corked the bottle and slid it into his hip pocket.

Will had his drink and got clumsily to his feet and had to put a hand to the chair back to steady himself. What the hell was the difference? He'd moved from place to place, dodging shadows; he'd worked his fool head off and hung onto a dream that made sense when he was sixteen, but always the deck got shuffled and the cards got cut against him. He looked at Buck. Buck was the only damned friend he had in the world, and just the other day he'd thought of running out on Buck. And right now he'd been telling Buck that he, William J. Yeoman, was too good for Buck's kind of pleasure. You could drown yourself just so deep in whiskey, and then the whiskey began to fail you, turning you sourer. Time to try something different.

"Let's go," Will said.

The outside air felt good on his face; a breeze moved across the Missouri and whispered in the cottonwoods along the bank, and that last steamer stood at the levee. That old packet better get started back downstream, Will decided, or it would find itself frozen in for the winter. He harked to the talk of the breeze — soft talk, not a bit scary. Once he'd stumbled along the Big Muddy's bank, hearing danger in every sound. Once a long, long time ago. Now the breeze sounded like music. Hell, that *was* music he was hearing! Coming from the grand ball they were holding in town tonight. He thought of Libbie Comfort who'd be dancing with some bigwig of the section, somebody like Brant Millard. He pushed the girl from his mind.

"This way," Buck said, getting Will's elbow and steering him.

Buck edged him around a corner and along a side street. Buck knew exactly where he was going. Damned if it wasn't good to have Buck running the show. Not a thing to worry about. They came to a clapboard building and let themselves into a dim hallway. A stairs reared upward, looking steep as a cliff. Will stumbled on the stairs, and Buck helped him to his feet.

Stumbling like that seemed funny to Will; it took him back to his last night in St. Louis. He heard himself ask, "Now who the hell built a horse-streetcar track on this stairs?"

"What you talking about?" Buck demanded.

"A horse-streetcar is a streetcar pulled by a horse," Will explained very profoundly.

They got to the top of the stairs and turned back along the upper hallway, also dimly lighted. Will said, "I can manage for myself," brushing aside Buck's arm. Buck moved to one of the several doorways that gave off the hall. He knocked on the door, and Will heard a faint stirring beyond the portal, and then the door opened and a frowsy-headed girl stood there. Her perfume was cheap and heavy and seemed to beat at Will.

The girl peered in the murkiness, then screamed, "Buck, honey!" She flung her arms around Buck's neck and at once began to draw him into the room.

Buck said, "I've got a friend with me, Trixie."

Trixie seemed to see Will for the first time. "The girl down at the end of the hall to your left is free," she said. "Go see her, cowboy."

The door closed behind the two. Will lurched on down the hall to the indicated door and stood before it. He raised his knuckles to rap upon the door, and a last misgiving crowded into his consciousness. This was not the way a man should first meet love, with a stranger and nothing lasting about it. This wasn't the way he had dreamed it would be. But what the hell had ever worked out the way it looked in a campfire?

It was hot in this hallway, stifling and oppressive. He wished he were out on the river bank where the breeze moved and the cottonwoods whispered. He thought he could hear faint strains of the music from the grand ball, a world away. He didn't remember willing himself to knock on the door, but he heard the drumming of his own knuckles.

The door opened, and in the first moment the girl was only a vagueness against the dim lamplight behind her, a perfumed shadow with a wrapper clutched loosely. She said, "Come in, honey," and it was her voice that turned him sober. A man might meet anybody in Fort Benton, he'd told himself. Anybody. She was eight years older and nearly the length of the Missouri from where she should have been, but she was Zoe.

8

Choice of Trails

The hotel bed was hard and lumpy, and Buck had opined as how they might have fared better by sleeping in the livery stable loft. Buck had done a lot of tossing and turning but now seemed settled down and maybe asleep. Not so Will. He lay flat on his back on his side of the bed, his hands locked at the nape of his neck; he lay staring at the dark ceiling overhead. Beyond these walls, Fort Benton had quieted down, its great roar broken into separate shards of sound that dwindled to echoes and were lost. The ball had broken up, Will judged, for he no longer heard the beat of music. An hour before he had listened to the last of the laughter and the grind of carriage wheels. The one window in this stuffy room should soon be showing the gray of dawn.

Will called softly "Buck — ?"

Buck rolled over. "Yeah?" Sleepily.

"I've been thinking. I'll string along with

you on that store deal."

Buck said in a livelier voice, "Good boy! I knew you'd make a pard to back a man. We'll work it out to a fine point tomorrow. Too tired now." He sighed; he seemed to doze for a moment. He said with sleepy satisfaction, "That Trixie! How was the girl you got, Will?"

"We only talked," Will said.

Buck came fully awake. "Only talked!" His voice was sharp with surprise. "Will, I'm damned if I understand you! I'm damned if I do."

"It doesn't matter," Will said tonelessly. "Go to sleep, Buck. We've got to rest. If we tackle that store job, we may do a lot of riding before we bed down again."

"That's right," Buck said. Soon he was snoring.

Will still stared at the ceiling. He knew that Buck must have been thinking that he, Will, hadn't had the nerve once they'd got to that place where Buck had taken him. Or maybe that Will, who hadn't at first warmed to the notion of going to visit the girls, had thought himself too good for store-bought love. He could side Buck in a holdup job, and he'd do it, come tomorrow, but he couldn't have told Buck how it had been in Zoe's room. It wasn't a thing for telling, but it was real enough in his mind — Zoe's not recognizing him there at the doorway the way he'd recognized Zoe, and her taking him by the arm and hauling him into the room and closing the door and saying, "Don't be afraid, honey. I'll show you a good time."

"Zoe," he'd said, half sick, "don't you know me?"

She'd looked at him a long moment by dim lamp-light, and then she'd known, and she'd laughed. That was the cruel part of it; she'd laughed. She'd been long at laughing, and then she'd said, "Men night after night until sometimes it seemed that every damn' man in the world had climbed those stairs. But the one I hadn't expected finally showed up. You, Will."

The rest of the talk was jumbled in his mind; but lying here in the hotel bed and sorting it out, he remembered asking her why she was here, and she'd told him about Carrico's place finally getting closed out by the law because there'd been too much cheating going on. For a while Carrico had gambled on the Missouri boats, and she'd worked with him, finding prospects among the passengers and sending them to Carrico's table. Fort Benton had been a final stop. Two years now she'd been in Benton.

"But this — ?" he'd asked, spreading his

hands to take in the cubicle of a room with its bed and stand and dim lamp burning.

"I've had to make a living somehow, Will."

Money? So he'd just put money into the mail for her at the old St. Louis address. Well, she'd waited a long time for money from him, but there hadn't been a smell of it. She'd got tired of waiting. Money in the mail now wouldn't do her any good, but she guessed her folks would find a use for it when it arrived. She said it with a shrug and a faint smile showing.

That was what had really got him, the way her whole attitude, even more than her words, insisted that what had happened to her was a natural thing, needing no defense. He'd got over the first shock of finding her here, but he couldn't get used to Zoe's showing indifference when his horror must be standing so plainly on his face. With his revulsion were anger and pity and regret. There had been more talk, none of it changing anything. And then, because there was nothing else left to say, he'd looked toward the door. "I guess I'd better be going, Zoe."

She came very close to him. She said in a soft voice, "I don't see why, Will."

And the hell of it was that he had still wanted her. In spite of everything. She was a woman now, more full-bodied than before;

and she had turned her sensuous face up to his, her red lips slightly parted, her lips willing. The dark cleft between her breasts showed, and the beginning of firm roundness. Her warmth drew him; she was desire. She was his first love, too, and the thought of her had walked between him and all the girls of all the towns.

But there were those stairs on which he had so recently stumbled, those stairs and the many boots that had beat against them; and so he'd said awkwardly, "I don't think so, Zoe. Not tonight, anyway," and she had laughed again.

"You'll come back, Will."

Outside, he'd found Buck. Buck had his shoulders against the wall and a cigarette burning in his face, and he said, "You sure took enough time," but Will had made no reply. They'd started along the street together, and at the corner they saw a carriage pulled up. As they drew abreast of it, the man inside had lighted a cigar, and his face had showed in the flare of the match. He was a man waiting, and Buck had grinned. "You see, Will, we pay our money to a girl, and she turns it over to another man. It's what you call a vicious circle."

He'd known at that moment, had Will, that he was going to side Buck in that holdup job tomorrow, though he hadn't said so. He'd had too damn' much for one day! First Mrs. Comfort and Libbie, and then Zoe, and now Carrico. Zoe hadn't mentioned what had become of Carrico after their Missouri packet days; she hadn't told him that she still worked for Carrico. But walking toward the hotel with Buck, he'd thought of what Buck had said about the name and the game. He was a marked man now, stripped of all the surety he'd gained in Pintoville by Lem Singleton's not recognizing him. Maybe Carrico and Zoe didn't know there was a murder charge hanging over him, but they knew the name Yeoman, and that made risk enough.

Would Zoe betray him, given the chance? He didn't suppose she would — they had been sweethearts once, and some measure of loyalty must still remain from the old days. But Carrico had surely hated him since that last night in St. Louis.

He thought of the question he'd once hoped to put to Carrico — the question that might have given him his real name. There could be no asking it without revealing himself and thus putting himself at Carrico's mercy. There was that hope he'd cherished about Zoe, and it lay dead. There was nothing left but to shake the dust of Benton. He could leave empty handed, if he still wished to hold to the old ideals that Zoe had shattered, or he could leave with pockets jingling as Buck wished.

Tomorrow . . .

He'd have to sleep. He turned on his side, putting his back to Buck, and willed himself to sleep. He began to doze, but the twilight of consciousness was thronged with the doings of the day — the ride along streets so brave with bunting, the climb to the depot site and all the oratory beneath the beating sun, the runaway, the saloon that evening, the stairs on which he'd stumbled . . . Out of this welter of remembered sounds and sights came an old recollection, and he heard clearly the voice of Matt Comfort on the St. Louis levee, speaking of Zoe and saying, "She's not for you." Now how could Comfort have guessed? Pondering, he drifted away . . .

Daylight stood bright against the window. Buck was seated on the edge of the bed, his head in his hands. Will said good morning to Buck. Buck said, "My mouth tastes like a bunch of sheepherders have been camping in it." He eased himself up with a groan and crossed to the bureau, a ludicrous figure in long underwear, with his shock of black hair standing every which way. He emptied the pitcher into the bowl and doused his head and managed a weak grin in Will's direction.

"What time is it?" Will asked.

"Around noon, I'd judge," Buck said. "So

124

much the better. Like I told you last night, we'd best hit that store near closing time. More money in the till then. It won't be much of a wait, seeing how many hours we've slept."

It all came back to Will then — the night and the drinking and Zoe and what he had promised Buck. He supposed his face must be showing some distaste, for Buck asked hastily, "You're still backing me, ain't you?"

"I'm still backing you," Will said. What had changed really? He flung the blankets aside. God, but this room looked dreadful, the wallpaper old and faded and stained, a fly-specked calendar tacked crookedly to the wall.

"Let's get some fresh air," Buck said.

They dressed and had something to eat and walked the streets. Bunting still festooned the buildings, and the sign hung across Main Street, and restaurant talk was all about the James J. Hill party's anticipated return from Great Falls; but Fort Benton, too, had awakened to a day less glorious than the one before.

Will wondered if Mrs. Comfort and Libbie were still in town, but he supposed they'd long since departed for Diamond C. He kept looking about for Zoe and Carrico, too. Would Carrico recognize him if they came face to face? He didn't know, and he wondered whether Zoe had told Carrico about who'd climbed the stairs last night; but he didn't catch a glimpse of either of them. Then, remembering his years at Carrico's place, he realized that those who work by night sleep by day.

Buck steered him toward the store he had in mind. It proved to be a small clothing store, catering to the trade of both men and women. Vacant lots flanked the building on either side, and Will judged that the isolation had been a strong factor in Buck's choice. They went inside, and Buck bought a neckerchief. A half dozen customers were in the place. Will stared about at the ceiling-high shelves but was quick to note that the coin Buck gave the proprietor went into a box placed under the counter. In addition to the proprietor, there was only one clerk, a pimply boy of about nineteen. Neither looked long on courage.

Outside, Buck took a look at the sun but shook his head. "Still too early," he said.

They walked along the river as far as the old adobe fort. Buck had been a cool one in the store, but he was beginning to show strain. He said brusquely, "Let's get our horses." They went to the livery stable and got saddled up, waving the old hostler aside and doing the chore themselves.

As they led their mounts along, Buck asked, "How much money you got left?" Will dug deep. Buck helped himself to some of the coins Will held forth. "We'll want grub rolled up in our slickers," Buck said. "You wait here." He went into Power's store.

Will held both horses and watched the flow of humanity along the street. The river ran close by, endlessly, timelessly. High above the bluffs a hawk circled. Buck came out with an armload and divided the supplies, and they stowed them away.

Buck took another look at the sun. "Let's go," he said.

They walked along, their horses plodding behind them; they walked toward the store. Buck's face grew taut. He spoke quick, clipped words. "I'll pretend to fix my cinch. You go on. Tie up before the store. Go inside. You're looking for a pair of pants, savvy. You don't like what they show you. Keep fiddling around till the other customers leave. Spin up a cigarette. When you've got the place to yourself, walk to the door and toss out the cigarette. Got that?"

Will nodded.

"I come in. You stay close to the door, Will. I'll throw a gun and hop over the counter and scoop up the money. Your job is to

keep an eye peeled for interference from outside. If anyone comes in, throw a gun on them
and line them up along the wall. The main
thing is not to get rattled. We move out fast.
We pile on our horses and cut north. Got
that?"

Again Will nodded.

They'd come abreast of the first of those vacant lots. Buck stopped, dropped the reins of
his horse, tossed back a stirrup and hooked it
over the saddle horn. He began fumbling at
the cinch. "Go on!" he said.

Will walked on to the store. He tied up his
horse, making sure the knot would slip easily,
and went inside. Two women were here; the
proprietor was waiting on one, his clerk on
the other. Will merely stood. The two women
chattered to each other as the two men pulled
merchandise from the shelves and piled it on
the counter for their inspection. Queer, Will
thought, how long it always took women to
make up their minds about a purchase. A
man, now, would point out what he wanted
and slap down the money. These women asked
each other's opinion, then asked to see more
merchandise. They kept up a conversation all
the while, the talk mostly about people of the
town.

Will looked about and smelled the woolly
smell of this place. How long could Buck stall

128

at pretending to fix a cinch? But Buck would find some other trick when the first one played out. Buck was a good hand at this sort of thing. For the first time, Will wondered if Buck had engineered other holdups.

His hands, he discovered, were sticky. He pulled them against his trouser legs. He wondered if his uneasiness stood out plain on his face and so could be read by the proprietor or his clerk if either of them chanced to look his way. His breath crowded his throat. And suddenly he was harked back in memory to another time when he'd had to flog his courage, that night at Carrico's when he'd nerved himself to quit the place. He supposed that again the trick was not to think of consequences. No fear of fist or lash this time, but of something else, of what all the years must hold when a man reached a fork in the trail and made such a choice as this.

One of the women was saying, " . . . I suppose you've seen that she's asking for help. Practically shameless about it. But it was bound to come. What business does a woman think she has trying to run a cattle ranch almost single-handed! It's ridiculous, I tell you."

"Hagar Comfort?" the other woman asked. "I hadn't heard."

"A paid advertisement in the *River Press*, no less. There's a copy on the counter. You can look for yourself."

Will saw the indicated paper. He sauntered toward it; he tried to look aimless, a man killing a little time. How long had he been in this store? Five minutes? Fifteen? He picked up the paper and moved back and opened it and began reading. A big to-do about the celebration, but he was seeking an obscure item. Finally he found the tiny, boxed-off notice. It read: "I am in need of help and am anxious to get in touch with any friends of my late husband, Matthew Comfort, who may chance to see this. Write to Mrs. Hagar Comfort, Diamond C Ranch, Fort Benton P. O."

He put the paper down and began walking toward the door. The clerk called after him, "Be free to help you in a minute," but Will said, "I'll drop in later." One of the women said, "My lands, these young people can't stand still a single second nowadays."

Will came out of the store. Buck was standing by his horse, looking intently toward the door, his face, hat shaded, full of worry and anger. Will untied his own horse and led it toward Buck. Buck asked petulantly, "What the hell's the matter?"

"I'm not going through with it, Buck," Will said.

Buck stared. "You're not going through with it!"

"That isn't all. We're splitting right here and now, Buck. You're taking your trail, and I'm taking mine. I've got a job to do. No, not the kind of job you think — not a deal like yonder store or a job with pay attached to it. Another kind of job. Something I can't turn my back on."

He lifted his free hand and let it fall, trying to put finality into the gesture. He realized how silly his speech must sound; he realized, as he'd realized so often before, how impossible it was to put into words for Buck the queer notions that were so singularly his own. How could he say that he'd just heard a call for help from one whose voice had been stilled for eight years but who now spoke through another? How could he tell Buck that after all his aimlessness he, Will, had been brought to a time and a place where existence at last made sense because a need had arisen, the need of another?

Buck said, "You're just walking out on me, is that it?"

"If you put it that way."

A mighty anger built in Buck, turning his sharp face tight, turning his eyes hard. Watching him, Will stiffened. He had known a drinking Buck, a rollicking Buck, and one with a tendency to such notions as had brought them before this store. Only now did he see that

131

there could be a dangerous Buck and that he was facing such a one. But his thought was that if Buck were to be the first obstacle standing between him and helping Hagar Comfort, then the fight must begin now. He was tensed for the fight, ready.

Then Buck smiled. "You're a queer galoot, kid," Buck said, "the queerest I've ever known. But we've ridden too many miles together for me not to give you the benefit of the doubt. Good luck wherever your trail takes you. Maybe we'll meet again."

"Good luck to you," Will said. He extended his hand and Buck took it. He smiled at Buck, trying to tell Buck with the smile that nothing sour lay between them, yet he wasn't sure. Not of Buck. Buck had smiled, too, but only with his lips. He still felt Buck's eyes on him after he'd brushed past Buck and started along the street, leading his horse and walking alone.

9

Fist and Boot

Will came back into the livery stable to find the hostler just lighting a lantern. Yellow glow flung itself into the corners but made the stalls more shadowy. The hostler placed the lantern upon a box and looked up at Will who stood silently on the splintered ramp. The hostler asked, "Forget something? I figured you'd be ten miles along the trail by now." He was a gnarled little man, this fellow, with the good smell of horses about him. Time had seamed his face, but his eyes were bright as any jay's.

Will said, "I thought I might hang around this part of the country."

"Where's that pard of your'n?"

"We've split our blankets. I think he's ridden out."

The hostler rubbed his chin. "You ain't of a kind. I opined that to myself when I first saw the pair of you. Dog and cat, I said."

Will shrugged. "Look, where can I find a

job in this section?"

"Riding? This ain't hiring time, kid. Them as is starting their roundups have got full crews."

"What about Diamond C?" Will asked. "I've heard of that outfit."

The hostler shook his head. "You're meaning Mrs. Comfort's place. Down the river a piece. She's hard pressed for cash. Her man used to have a store here. The missus sold the store years ago and put the money into blooded stock on the ranch. Comfort's dead. Got killed on a river packet by some hellion of a kid he'd taken under his wing. That was Matt Comfort for you; he couldn't pass up a kicked dog. This one had sharp teeth."

"So you don't think she'd be hiring?"

"Not likely. She's had a lot of trouble ever since she started. Rustlers seem to fancy that blooded stuff of hers, and bad luck just naturally dogs Diamond C."

"Neighbors bothering her?"

Again the hostler shook his head. "Not that I've heard. The closest one she's got is Brant Millard with his B-M Connected outfit, and he's got no need to be rustling. Besides, he's courting the Comfort girl. Say, Millard keeps a big crew. You might stand a chance there."

"Can you draw me a map showing the way?"

The hostler found a scrap of paper and a stub of pencil. He spread the paper out on the top of the box which held the lantern. "This here's the river," he said as he drew a wriggly line. "And this here is Fort Benton, see. Shonkin Creek comes in about here, and the Teton and the Marias join up about here and empty into the Big Muddy." He added other landmarks and identified them. "Now here" — he marked a spot on the Missouri with an awkward X — "is Diamond C. And here's Millard's place."

Will took the map, folded it, and put it into his shirt pocket. "Two more things. Can I have the loan of a currycomb, and can I bunk in the hayloft tonight?"

"You'll find a currycomb laying around somewhere, and yonder's the ladder to the loft."

"I'm much obliged," Will said. "For everything."

His horse worked over and his blanket spread in the hay, Will lay in the rustling darkness of the loft an hour later and made his plans. When he'd walked away from Buck in the late afternoon, he'd wanted to go directly to Mrs. Comfort in the manner of a man, hand outstretched and hat off. But first he'd needed to locate Diamond C, and he'd thought of the hostler and so headed for the livery stable soon after he'd eaten. What the hostler had told him had suggested a plan.

It added up to meeting each circumstance as it shaped itself. The hostler had said that the Comforts weren't likely hiring. He couldn't go to Diamond C as a friend of Matt Comfort's who'd seen the notice in the paper, not when he couldn't explain how that friendship had come about. Nor could he go as a wandering ranny in search of a place to rest his saddle, especially since they'd be obligated to make him welcome because of his stopping that runaway. He didn't like the notion of trading on that incident. Thus if he were to get close enough to the Comforts to find the source of their trouble, he'd have to locate himself on one of the nearby ranches.

The map had given him his cue. Millard's B-M, much larger than Diamond C, abutted the Comfort place. From B-M a man could size up the situation in the neighborhood. But now a new thought struck him. Was the bad luck that dogged the Comforts calculated to drive them off their land? If so, Brant Millard might stand to gain by gobbling up his neighbor. But the hostler hadn't any such suspicion, and Will remembered Millard's show of concern about the Comforts after the runaway. Hardly the attitude of a man carrying on an undercover range war. And the hostler had said that Millard was courting Libbie Comfort. Could the man be scheming to marry Diamond C's land?

Will shook his head at his own imaginings, remembering the Ned Buntline thrillers he'd once read. He had nothing, really, to make a case against Millard. He wanted to roll over and ask Buck what he thought about it all, but Buck wasn't here.

Suddenly he missed Buck, missed him mightily, even though he'd always had to guard his tongue around Buck and pull Buck back by the shirttail from some of Buck's wild notions. He wondered where Buck rode tonight and if they'd meet again. For a fact, trails kept crossing.

This swung his mind to Zoe. The pain of last night's discovery was now only a numbness that lay heavily within him. Maybe there was an excuse for Zoe, all things considered. Probably a good deal of the blame lay with himself for not having been able to send for her as he'd planned. Yet surely she could have found another way of making a living. But when he pinned the whole thing down, he found a core of selfishness in his feelings. It hurt a man's pride to think of all the other men there'd been. What of Zoe, who'd had to live it all? Damn Carrico for dragging her down! Thinking thus, he drifted into sleep . . .

He was on the trail while the grass still lay wet with dew and the meadow larks caroled. He headed west a short ways, following the storied Whoop-Up Trail, where once a liquor trade had flourished and in later days the North West Mounted Police had sent their recruits and supplies overland to their Canadian outposts until the newly-built Canadian Pacific Railway took away the traffic. The old ruts still showed, but Will soon left them, taking the high lift of the Bear Paws to the north for his landmark. History there, too, he reflected, for just a few days shy of ten years ago, Chief Joseph of the non-treaty Nez Perces had ended a war by handing his rifle in surrender to Colonel Miles.

A land that had known violence, this, and the dark strain was still here. Likely there'd be violence before his job was done, and he was glad he possessed a gun and the skill to use it, though he was not as proficient as Buck, who'd grown up with a six-shooter. He put his mind away from this kind of thinking, finding it out of tune with the day. He rode across a vastness of land and was reminded that this Chouteau County, of which Fort Benton was the county seat, was said to be the largest county in the United States. Range country always got him by the throat with its wide sweep, its far horizons. He wondered about this, feeling at times strangely come home as though he belonged here and had known all this before.

He was a man whose thoughts had turned inward all his solitary years, and those years included St. Louis, where he'd known the peopled nights of Carrico's place but still stood alone. It came to him now that when he searched himself, he was also searching out his own kin. Another man could lay claim to temper because his Uncle Jeb had been a hot-headed one, or like apple pie because his mother could never get her fill of it, and so all men were made up of the fragmentary parts of the people who had come before them and created them out of their passion. He, too, therefore must have his inheritance, and the difference was that he had to find it within himself, having no kin to whom he could trace his likes and his dislikes.

Take that matter of temper. It could come up in him like a flame, but afterward he could ponder it. Anger had ridden him as he lay on the floor of Carrico's place, and the same anger had been his when felled by another fist in the blacksmith shop at Pintoville. Who had given him anger and how had that other man, that unknown one who had been on a steam-boat at Lexington, fared with it?

Always there were such questions, and so

he rode, busy with his fancies; he came across the face of the land, with the big sky over him and the earth drumming to the beat of his horse's hoofs; he came to B-M Connected.

He rode in with the sun telling him the afternoon was well started, and he found the ranch buildings sheltered by a high bluff. There was a sprawling house of log and frame with a gallery fronting it, a bigger barn, a good-sized bunkhouse, a cook-shack, several other buildings. The crew, it seemed, was out on the range, for he saw only one man as he approached. That man was standing in a breaking corral. He had a wild-eyed stallion snubbed close to the post, and he was laying a blacksnake across the horse with insane fury.

And the anger came rising in Will again, engulfing him.

The shaggy black coat of the horse glistened redly; the animal struck out with flailing hoofs, but the man was keeping at a safe distance. He stood with his back to Will, his arm raising and pistoning forward with frenzied regularity, this action sending the lash singing and drawing the man's shirt tight. An expanse of sweat darkened his shirt.

Will reined closer and called out, "Your private horse, mister?"

The man now became aware of Will for the

first time. He swung around, revealing himself to be heavyset and slightly stooped and truculent of jaw. He had the kind of blue stubble no razor could truly erase. Near forty, Will judged, and sensed that he'd seen him before; he supposed probably the fellow had been with Millard. The man drew a sleeve across his forehead.

"He's a B-M horse," the man said, "and I'm Blucher, foreman here. What business is it of yours?"

Will said, "Whatever the horse did, he's had enough. Do you want to kill him?"

Blucher said, "He'll break to saddle or I'll kill him. The choice is his." He swung around and sent the blacksnake singing again.

Will came down from his saddle. Something in him whispered that he tread carefully, but he was deaf to the whisper. It was the whip that moved him; he had tasted a whip. The corral gate was open, and he walked inside. He came up to Blucher and got him by the shoulder and swung the man around. Then Will hit him.

The blow took the legs out from under Blucher and dumped him into the dust, but he came up at once and raised the blacksnake. His face showing fury, he sent the whip lashing at Will. Will got under the whip and closed with Blucher and wrenched the whip away and flung it aside. Blucher got a leg behind Will and, straining, tripped him, and the two went down together. Rolling in the dust, Will was too angry for straight thinking till he realized they were almost under the stallion's driving hoofs. The thunder of those hoofs gave him his warning.

Writhing clear, he dragged Blucher to his feet. The whip lay nearby, and with a lurching movement, Will picked it up. A kind of madness was in him. He got Blucher by the collar and hauled him from the corral and then sent Blucher away from him with a shove of his free hand. He swung the whip, laying it twice across Blucher's shoulders.

"Now you try a taste of it!" Will panted.

Blucher made a harsh animal sound and came at him. Will flung the whip far aside and met that rush with upraised fists. The fury of Blucher's drive bowled him over, and Blucher kicked at him. Will caught the man's boot and twisted, dumping Blucher. They both came to their feet at once and started for each other. Will got in under Blucher's charge and gave the man punishment. He saw Blucher's eyes grow dark and savage; Blucher now remembered the gun that swung at his hip and tried for it. Will closed with him, pinioning Blucher's arms. They stood locked together, straining and tugging, but Will managed to lift Blucher's gun from leather and throw it aside. Then he stepped back from Blucher and it became a slugging match.

In Will a small regret clamored. He'd come here to get a job, and now he found himself battling the B-M foreman, thereby smashing down his own chance. But there could be no stepping out of the fight now. The two went slugging across the yard. Will's advantage was youth, but Blucher's was weight, and it was anybody's fight. This Blucher was a hard one, but he began to show that he didn't have the staying power. Soon Will had him sobbing for breath. Seeing this, Will pinned his faith in footwork and became a hard man to find and a harder one to hit. Thus, gradually, he wore Blucher down. And then Will became conscious that there was a spectator to the fight.

Brant Millard had come around a corner of the ranch house, drawn, probably, by the sound of the fracas. He merely stood watching. He stood with his feet spread apart and his arms folded, a slight smile showing. Even when Blucher, panting and desperate, shouted, "Brant! Gun the man down! For God's sake, gun him down!" Millard made no move.

Blucher, turning his head to make that appeal, had left his jaw unguarded, and Will struck hard. The shock of the blow drove up to his elbow, but in the sting of his knuckles against Blucher's chin, he found a primitive delight. Blucher swung his arms wide and flailed wildly, trying to get a hold on the air. Then he went down, stunned and bleeding and just barely clinging to consciousness. He fell on his back, sighed and rolled over; and all the fight was gone out of him.

Will towered over him. "Had enough?" Will demanded and stood with fists cocked. The earth seemed to be lurching, and the nearby corral appeared to buck and heave.

Brant Millard answered for Blucher. "He's had more than enough, I'd say."

Will shook his head and so managed to make his eyes focus. This was his first real fist fight, and he knew that he'd won it by a mighty narrow margin. He drew in a breath, the effort driving pain deep into him. He got a real look at Millard now. The man had thumbed back his wide hat, thus revealing gray-streaked black hair. A big man and a handsome one in a bluff sort of way. He wore range garb, but his fitted breeches had never polished a saddle for sixteen hours at a stretch. In his prime, still Millard was obviously old enough to be Libbie Comfort's father. Will didn't warm to the man. Millard had drawn a peculiar pleasure out of watching the fight; even now there was no pity in him for his beaten foreman.

Anger still burned in Will. "Was he whipping that horse by your order?" he demanded.

Millard shrugged. His were heavy eyelids that gave him a perpetually sleepy look. "The blacksnake was his own idea," Millard said. "That's why I didn't interfere between the two of you. It was a personal fight."

"Just the same, you didn't come out to stop him!" Will insisted hotly.

Millard made a movement with his hands. "Look," he said in a patient voice, "that's over and done with. You've squared for the horse, from the looks of my man. Now hadn't you better be saying what fetched you here?"

"I was looking for a job."

Millard's glance moved to Will's horse, which stood with reins trailing. A rancher usually sized up a man's mount, and from its appearance as often as not made his judgment of the man. But that currycomb job was wasted, for Millard's real interest seemed to be only in the brand the bay wore. Two Cross was a far piece from here and gone out of business besides.

Millard said, "I remember you from Benton, of course. A drifter, I take it. Your name?"

Will's face hardened. "Do you hire names, or men, on this ranch?"

Was it a new appreciation that showed suddenly in Millard's sleepy eyes? "Maybe I can use you," he said. "Maybe I can, at that."

Blucher raised himself up on one elbow. He lifted a battered, broken face. "Hire him, Brant, and I roll my soogans! B-M Connected is big — but not big enough for the two of us!"

Millard sent him a stern look, and Will judged there was a message in it, mute but commanding. "No, Henry, you'll be staying," Millard said. His glance moved back to Will. "And you, Slim, take your fixings to the bunkhouse. Turn your horse into one of the corrals. The crew should be in about sundown. We have supper then."

Millard turned and walked toward the ranch house. In this manner had Will Yeoman found himself hired by B-M Connected. He limped to where Blucher lay and offered his hand to help the man to his feet, but Blucher shook his head angrily and arose under his own power and lurched to where Will had thrown the gun. Will eyed him closely, but Blucher cased the gun and headed toward the bunkhouse.

Will shrugged and picked up the bay's reins. Last night, in the livery hayloft, he'd wondered if Brant Millard might bear watching, but that notion had been based on nothing solid. Now he was sure that Millard had hired him for the very reason that most ranchers would have turned him away — his pointed refusal to hang a name on himself, his tacit hint that his backtrail was shadowy.

This ranch had an undercurrent that Will was already sensing. He'd do well to watch his step.

10

Libbie

The crew came in an hour this side of sundown, and Will put his appraisal on them and grew more curious about this ranch. There were too many men for the size of the spread, and they were a hardcase bunch from the looks of them, more skilled with the six-shooter than with rope and branding iron. They made a great show of arriving; they whirled into the yard, stirring the dust, then lighted down and began peeling gear from their horses. They hadn't put in a hard day at work, not with this much zip left.

When they began to dribble toward the bunkhouse, where Will sat on a bench outside the door waiting, they favored him with quick, calculating glances and curt nods but otherwise ignored him. They came tall and short, broad and lean, but there was no fun in them, no easiness. This B-M Connected obviously knew none of the hoorawing and good fellowship of most ranches.

The fact was borne out when they all trooped into the cook-shack to seat themselves around a long table for a supper that was eaten in surly silence. Afterward, when they were congregated in the bunkhouse, someone suggested a poker game. Five of the dozen men got into it, but nobody asked Will to play, and for awhile he stood watching the game. They used match sticks for chips and set a four-bit value on them, mighty high stakes for a bunkhouse game.

Blucher was here, busying himself at braiding a quirt, making very sure he had his eyes down whenever Will happened to glance his way. One of the crew, noticing Blucher's battered face at the supper table, had put a question to the foreman and got only a grunt in reply. There'd been no further reference to the fight that Blucher had so obviously been in, but there were telltale marks on Will's face, too, and the crew must have drawn its conclusions.

Will had found an unused bunk for himself and dumped his gear upon it. While the poker game was still in progress, he undressed down to his underwear and climbed into the bunk and lay there smoking, his hands hooked at the back of his neck. In late evening the game broke up noisily; one by one the men sought their blankets. When all were bedded down, someone called, "Hey, you, new feller. Blow out the lamp."

Will said in a flat voice, "I wasn't the last one in. Blow it out yourself."

Someone else said sleepily, "Quit the damn' jawing! How does a man get any rest around here?" Still another man climbed from his bunk with an oath. He padded across the floor to the table, bent over the lamp and extinguished it.

Grass-filled ticks rustled to the movement of men's bodies. In the darkness someone said, "Another day — another dollar. Now what the hell did I do with last summer's pay?" Far beyond the ranch buildings a coyote howled mournfully, and in a nearby corral a horse stomped. That whip-seared stallion? A man cursed as he rolled over in his bunk, and Will recognized Henry Blucher's voice.

Blucher was feeling mighty sore of bone and muscle tonight, Will bet. He'd felt the foreman's hate all of this evening, like an extra presence in the bunkhouse. Will reached out now and touched the butt of his gun in its holster; he'd hung belt and holster on a peg by the bunk. He was tempted to take the gun and slip it into the blankets beside him. He decided against this. Such a maneuver would be recognized when he retrieved the gun in the morning. He'd shown them all his measure when he'd refused to blow out the lamp. Contempt would make a stronger armor than caution.

So thinking, he slept . . .

He awoke to find himself stiff from what Blucher's fists had done to him; his first movement sent a dull agony all through him. The bunkhouse was astir, and he saw that Blucher, too, moved painfully. They all went out to have a turn at the washbasins, but Will was the only one who took time to shave. He came late to the cook-shack, but the cook, a grizzled old man, had saved breakfast for him. "Shaved, huh!" the cook observed. "What office you running for?" Oddly, these were the friendliest words Will had heard on this ranch.

Afterward Will joined the crew in the yard and was loitering with them when Millard came striding from the house.

Millard looked them over, his eyes pausing on Blucher. Something cat-like showed in Millard's glance. "Henry, I imagine you'll want another try at breaking El Capitan." He said this without smiling.

Blucher looked toward the breaking corral, and the whites of his eyes were plainly revealed. "Goddam it, Brant, I won't go near that murdering brute!"

Millard said, "Take about five of the boys and do some line-riding. I'll want to know where most of the stock is scattered before we get started on fall roundup. I'd like a rough count on the weaners, too."

Blucher gestured to the men standing nearest him, and this little group headed away to saddle up. Millard studied the others. "You, Chase," he said to one, "can help the coosie overhaul the chuck wagon. Noonan, you'd better give him a hand, too. Beal, there are a couple of seep springs that need digging out. The rest of you can work on gear. I don't want a lot of broken leather and snapped ropes when we get the roundup going."

His gaze moved to Will. "Slim, I've got a special chore for you."

Will stood idly, studying Millard as a couple of the men stopped to ask the B-M boss for more specific orders. A hard one to pigeonhole, this Millard. No Texan, apparently, come up with the trail herds to found a new empire on Montana's hills, for no pad of a Texas drawl clung to Millard's tongue. No Easterner, either, at least not one of the more recent ones sent out to run syndicate-owned ranches, such as Bar B on the Musselshell. Yet this B-M Connected seemed to have money behind it, either Millard's own or that of big investors. Was Millard another Fort

Benton merchant turned rancher?

Millard, free of his men, again put his sleepy gaze upon Will. "You remember Mrs. Comfort?"

Will chose to look blank.

"The lady whose buggy you stopped the day of the silver spike celebration. Her Diamond C lies yonder." He waved in the direction of the river. "I want you to ride over there today. You're to carry a message. Tell her if she needs help on her fall roundup to let me know and I'll send as many of my men as she wants. Do you understand?"

Will nodded.

"If you keep moving toward the river, you can't miss the place."

"Sure," Will said.

Millard turned and strode back toward the ranch house. Walking across the yard, he made a good figure of a man, tall and broad shouldered and well proportioned. Will watched him go and then went about getting gear onto the bay. He climbed to saddle and rode by the breaking corral where the great black stallion roved about. El Capitan laid back his ears and pawed a bit of dirt, thus making his challenge. Will said, "You keep fighting, old son."

He rode out of B-M's yard then and headed in a straight line toward the river, coming soon into the breaks. He rode slowly, favoring his bruised body. Blucher, not as tall as Will, had done most of his damage to Will's ribs, not marking his face much. It almost hurt to breathe, but Will judged no ribs were broken. His lips felt puffy, and some skin had been rubbed off one cheekbone.

He had to concede that a man wasn't asked to strain himself, working for the ol' B-M. The question was strong in him, though, as to why he'd been picked for this task. Any other hand would have qualified and considered it a holiday to be sent on so simple a mission on such a day as this, for it was another good one, golden and sun livened. Most owners would have put a new man at work calculated to make him familiar with the ranch. Was this a kindness because Millard realized that he, Will, wasn't feeling too perky after that fight yesterday? Will wasn't sure. He supposed he shouldn't quarrel with good fortune, yet he kept wondering why he'd been chosen. He finally pushed the question aside as unanswerable.

Far out from B-M, he found a small spring seeping from the ground, and here he watered the bay and had a drink for himself. It was near enough to noon so that he was beginning to feel hungry. He rode on. Shortly thereafter he saw the lift of smoke from a chimney and began following a draw that widened out as he drew near the river. In the openness at the draw's end, he came upon Diamond C's buildings.

The house was log with a dirt roof and no gallery, and the barn wasn't very big but wore fresh red paint. The bunkhouse was about the size of B-M's wagon shed. The corrals were all in good repair, and the entire place looked tidy. Drawing nearer, he saw curtains at the windows of the house and rock-bordered flowers growing bravely by the walk leading to the front door. A petticoat ranch, for sure. All the signs of feminine influence interested him; they were expressions of the personality of the two who'd fashioned this place out of Matt Comfort's dreaming. Beyond, the river shone in the sunlight, and for a moment he felt very near to Matt.

Libbie came to the doorway as he rode up. He drew rein and said, "I come from B-M Connected, Miss."

She had been baking, he judged, for there was a smear of flour on her cheek. She regarded him with a frown. "I remember you now," she said. "The man who stopped the runaway." She looked at him more intently. "What happened to your face?"

"An argument," Will said.

She made a small gesture with her hand. "Would you like to light?"

"I only came to deliver a message to your mother. Is she here?"

"She went to town this morning," Libbie said. "If it's all the same to you, I'll take the message."

She wasn't a pretty girl, Will decided. Not near as pretty as Zoe. She was wearing an apron over butternut britches today, and she had on a man's plaid shirt. Her reddish-brown hair hung in two braids down her back and was drawn back from a face so frank that it might have been a boy's. Although that bridge of freckles was gone from across her nose, he saw now that the faint shadow of them still lingered. But the thing that struck him the hardest was the faint animosity that marked her whole attitude. It hadn't showed so much in what she'd said but in the tone she'd used, and there was that frown.

He said, "Brant Millard says if you need help on the roundup, he'll send as many men as you want."

Her lips drew to a severe line just as they had outside Fort Benton when Millard had offered to drive the buggy the rest of the way to Diamond C. "You can tell Brant Millard," she said, "that it's high time he learns that the way to a girl's heart is not through a roundup crew!"

"I'll repeat it word for word," Will said.

Her frown deepened, and then she laughed. With her laughter her face showed a radiance that changed her completely. "Do you know," she said, "I believe you will. What's more, I believe you'll get pleasure from it."

"All in the day's work," Will said.

She dusted her hands on her apron. "The crew should be in for dinner any time now. We have only a small outfit, so we eat in the house. You can stay if you like. There's a wash basin on the bench outside the bunkhouse."

"I'll stay," he decided and swung down.

She came and took the reins and began to lead his horse toward the barn. He fell in beside her. He was deeply interested in her; she was Matt Comfort's daughter. She had a firm, boyish stride, but she was a girl for all that, high breasted and graceful of hip. He found himself wondering how it would be if someone hauled off and kissed her. He could imagine that face turning slack with surprise, then stiffening with anger; but he judged there'd be no scratching or slapping or fainting away. The man would probably get a good punch in the nose from a doubled-up fist.

Into the barn's cool darkness, she slapped the bay into a stall and began working at the cinch, preparatory to unsaddling. Will stepped beside her. "Here, I can do that," he said.

157

That faint animosity showed again. "Do you think I'm not able?"

He shrugged. "Just loosen the cinch. No need to haul off the hull."

He left the barn and strode to the bunkhouse and washed up. She lifted a hand to him as she came back across the yard. "I've got things on the stove," she called.

"Looks like your crew's coming in," he observed. A small group of horsemen were single filing down the slanted side of the draw.

"Trail along with me if you want to be of help," she said.

He followed her into the house. It had no more than three or four rooms, he judged, and the kitchen was the largest and accommodated a big table. He passed through a comfortably furnished living room to reach the kitchen. Libbie busied herself at the stove, and he set the table according to her instructions. Six places in all. Heat crowded from the stove, and Libbie's face grew red from the heat, but she did not slacken her pace, moving from stove to table and back again. Will was clattering away with the last of the knives and forks when he heard the mutter of boots beyond the kitchen door and the men came crowding in together.

The first was a wizened Mexican, and Libbie said, "This is Pablo."

158

"They call me Slim," Will said.

A tall, stoop-shouldered man, well into his sixties was introduced next — his name was Rube Freeman — and then a lad no more than sixteen, tow headed and weak chinned. "Lum Garvey," Libbie said. "And of course you already know Buck."

"Sure," said Buck Harper with a grin. "How are things, *Slim?*"

"Fair to middling," Will said, but he knew his surprise showed.

They sat down at the table. Libbie served them and then seated herself, too. Pablo's only speech was to request the passing of the pepper, and Rube Freeman occupied himself with eating. The boy Lum spoke enthusiastically about the morning's work, but after that one outburst had no more to say. Buck, though, kept up a running talk. Will listened without really hearing him. He was thinking that Buck had made himself mighty at home in the very short time since he'd signed on here.

The meal over, they all trooped outside. Will paused at the kitchen door. "I'll be getting back," he said to Libbie, who'd been collecting dishes from the table. "I'm obliged for a prime meal." He held out his hand to her. She shook hands. Then she said, "You don't like him, do you?"

He shook his head, not understanding.

"Buck," she said. "You were together at Fort Benton the other day. He told us you'd been saddle pards for quite some time. But I watched you at table and saw the way you stared at him."

He said, "Buck's all right," and went on outside.

The others were saddling up. He went to the barn and drew the cinch tight on the bay and led his mount into the yard. He found Diamond C's crew up into leather and ready to ride out. He called, "Just a minute, Buck."

Buck waved to the others to go on. He rode over to where Will stood and looked down at Will from his saddle. "Some surprised, eh, kid?"

"Some," Will admitted. "What fetched you here, Buck?"

"A place to roundside," Buck said. "You didn't seem interested in following up on the gratitude that was likely to be flowing around here. I saw no harm in moving in."

Will said, "I was told this place wasn't hiring."

"They're short of cash, but I said I'd be willing to string along until their roundup gather gets sold. It adds up to three squares meanwhile and a wall against those winter winds that are going to be blowing shortly.

Besides, there's the girl."

Will said flatly, "What about her, Buck?"

Buck grinned. "She makes out to be nail-hard and a man-hater from away back. It's mostly show, Will. What she's really aching for, even though she hasn't found it out yet, is a bit of loving. I think I'll stick around."

Will reached up and got hold of Buck's shirt front and took a good bunch of it in his fist and twisted hard. He said, "Buck, if you do that girl or her mother any kind of harm, I'll tack your hide to a tree!"

Buck's grin faded, and a cold deadliness came into his eyes. He batted at Will's hand, and Will let go his grip. Buck said, "We've ridden a lot of miles together, Will, but that doesn't give you leave to lay a hand on me or tell me how I'm to conduct myself. All I'll ever get from that girl, or any, is what she's willing to give. What the hell is it to you?"

Will said, "I'm thinking that you're no damn' good, Buck."

"Well," Buck said pointedly, "I'm not on the dodge. Not yet, anyway."

"No," Will said. "You're not." He swung up to his saddle and reined his horse about. Anger was again beating in his temples. He would have ridden away, but he heard Buck call his name. He turned and saw that the coldness was no longer in Buck's eyes.

"I don't like parting this way, Will," Buck said. "I guess maybe these people here mean something special to you. I got that notion right after you stopped that runaway. I'm not asking any questions, and I'll not bother the girl any. Now how about that? No hard feelings, kid?"

"Not till you give me reason," Will said. He touched steel to the bay and rode out.

11

Back to Benton

October had come, and roundup time.

By day the sunlight lay thin and sharp on the land, turning it golden, turning it mellow; by night the wild geese wedged across a darkling sky and showered the earth with their weird calling. Where trees clustered, they had taken on fall colors and some were shedding leaves to pile a rustling carpet on the prairie's rim. The mornings were crisp with a hint of frost; ice rimmed water buckets and creek edges, and there were squally days of leaden skies and rain that held a sting and often turned to snow. And so the world showed changing moods, sometimes brooding with Indian summer's sadness, sometimes racketing with the promise of winter.

With B-M Connected's crew, Will worked long hours. Theirs was a localized roundup, with not even a rep sent to cut out B-M strays from Diamond C's gather, or any of the crew showing from the river ranch to perform a similar service.

Will had grown to like the spring roundups he had known on the other ranches, especially since the formation of the Territorial Stock-growers Association three years before, which had resulted in the dividing of the cattle country into districts and the roundups' being conducted large scale, with the crews of many ranches under a single captain. Made quite a show, those doings. Often there was a dance the night before the start and then a horseback parade to the rendezvous where the roundup really began, the ladies riding along as far as the first camp. There was plenty of pageantry and color and zest, and the feel in a man that he was mixed into big doings. Fall roundups were never so fancy, but this one at B-M began to strike Will as a mockery.

True, the riders were in saddle early and late, and they combed all the wide country for strays, Blucher bellowing orders and the men sweating under the sun or beating their way through the rain. Branding fires burned, and the stench of singed hair and hide arose as calves that had been missed in the spring roundup were roped for the iron. Strays were hazed toward a bedding ground not far from the ranch buildings and held there against a time when the marketable beef would be cut out for shipment and sale.

But none of this was done with any real enthusiasm. These were wooden men, jerked by the string of Blucher's voice. No one paid much heed when a passing rider fetched news from town that the Manitoba was doing everything in its power to accommodate shippers. He said that permanent shipping pens would at once be constructed both at the Teton and on the hill near the Benton depot site.

It was as though B-M went through the motions of a roundup without anyone really caring. Not even Brant Millard, who scarcely showed himself, though sometimes he rode to the bedding ground, had a sleepy glance at the gather, asked a question or two, and then turned back to the comforts of his ranch house.

The herd itself was no proof of pride in ownership, a mixture of scrub cattle and imported stuff, with quite a bit of longhorn strain evident. Here, too, was a mockery — a big ranch, a prosperous appearing ranch, with beef that the average two-bit squatter would have scorned. Not even the hard winter that had devastated the range could account for the poor showing of B-M's stock.

All of which added new aspects to the riddle that was B-M Connected, but the days gave no answer to that riddle, and sometimes

Will wondered if he were wasting his time. His objective was still simple and clear: he was out to aid Mrs. Comfort by finding who was behind the trouble that had caused her to cry for help. After that, his next step would be to stop the trouble. In Fort Benton he'd had that faint suspicion that B-M might be engineering the rustling. He'd decided that his suspicion was ridiculous. Now he was even more convinced. Brant Millard had no need to be rustling, the hostler had declared. And now Millard was proving that he wasn't interested in his own stock, much less in his neighbors'. There was that offer of Millard's to lend roundup help to Diamond C, and certainly no men rode from B-M on midnight raids. From the higher ridges Will sometimes glimpsed Diamond C's crew also on roundup; and all seemed serene.

Once he was sure he recognized Buck working a distant hogback for the river ranch. He'd thought a lot about Buck since that day he'd braced Buck in Diamond C's yard. Libbie had accused him of not liking Buck. He wondered if this were so. He had Buck's parting words to remember — the renewed offer of friendship. But Buck could be almighty quick with the smooth talk and the warm smile. The question was how much sincerity there was in Buck. No denying that Will hadn't been pleased to find Buck at Diamond C's table; and later he hadn't leaped at Buck's efforts to pacify him. Yet if there were ever a showdown in the trouble that beset the Comforts, it might be well to have someone at Diamond C as cool and tough as Buck in a tight.

Trouble was, there seemed to be no showdown shaping, and always Will's thinking swung back to the greater question — was he wasting his time?

He clung to patience. He had learned patience with a gold pan in his hands along the mountain streams; he had learned patience through a winter when he'd ridden with eyes lamp-soot blackened against snow-blindness and his feet gunny sack encased to keep out the freezing cold, ridden in futile fight against the winter's white inroads on cattledom. He would be patient again. All the days could not be like these roundup days with their rush and roar that still contrived to be empty of purpose.

And on a morning at the bedding grounds, Blucher summoned him by a gesture of his hand. Blucher had ridden to the ranch the night before and stayed to sleep in the bunkhouse. Blucher said, "The boss wants to see you."

Will nodded. In his several days on the ranch, the crew had become names and individuals to him — Noonan and Beal and Case, Moffat and Grant and the eternal Tex, a Yellowstone Kid and a Marias Kid, and the others. But he had grown no closer to them for all the small familiarities that grew out of association. He could borrow the tobacco of any one, but he got not so much as a crumb of their confidence. From Blucher he'd had nothing but orders, and they were always the hardest orders, sending him into the most difficult country to do a day's hazing. Blucher hated him, he knew, but the man made a great show of ignoring him outside of the normal contacts called for by work. Perhaps Blucher clung to patience, too.

Saddling up, Will rode to a ranch yard that looked almost ghostly in its desertion, with the crew gone and the corrals empty of spare horses. No smoke lifted from the cook-shack, for the coosie was with the chuck wagon out on the range, and only a thin blue wisp showed above the chimney of the ranch house. By that token, Will judged that Brant Millard was in the building. Millard had never asked him into the house, so he alighted in the yard, knowing that Millard would see him. Only one living thing showed to Will, the stallion El Capitan in the breaking corral.

Will walked toward the corral, pulled by both fear and fascination. That brute of a cayuse was an engine of destruction, but he was also a thing of beauty. He'd been one of a band of wild horses the B-M crew had rounded up in the Marias breaks the spring before, Will had learned, the only one as yet unbroken to saddle. Today El Capitan looked almost asleep on his feet.

Drawn in spite of himself, Will gingerly opened the corral gate, slipped inside, and closed the gate after him. At once El Capitan's head came up. Will took a step toward the stallion and spoke soothingly. El Capitan snorted, laying back his ears and showing wild, white eyes. In Will good sense screamed that he get out of the corral, but something beyond reason kept him there. He willed himself to another step forward, his hand out and his voice soft and assuring. The stallion came at him then, charging and trumpeting and looming bigger than anything in the world.

Will bolted for the fence and clawed his way high, hearing the thud of that great body against the poles. The shock of the assault almost broke Will's hold.

From below, Brant Millard said, "So you feel a challenge in him, too."

Will looked down from where he straddled the top rail to see Millard standing just beyond the corral. Will dropped to the ground on the outside. El Capitan was circling the corral, kicking up the dust. Will said, "I don't think anyone will ever ride him."

"Perhaps not," Millard said. He gazed at the horse reflectively. "Or it will be a desperate man who does. A man more desperate than the horse."

Will said, "You wanted me."

This was the first time he'd exchanged words with Millard since that day, nearly a week before, when he, Will, had returned from Diamond C. As he'd promised Libbie, he'd delivered her reply to Millard word for word. Millard had stood on the gallery of the ranch house and received the message. For a moment his ponderous jaw had tightened, and a muscle along it had twitched. Then he'd looked at Will in his sleepy way. "And what did you say to that, Slim?"

"I told her I'd tote her message."

Millard said sharply, "But perhaps it pleased you to hear such a rebuff!"

Will had shrugged. "All in the day's work."

Whereupon Millard had looked at him long and appraisingly and at last turned back into the house. Now, here by the corral, Millard gave him that same searching look, then reached into his pocket and produced a stamped envelope. "I want this in the Fort Benton post office today. See that it gets there."

"Sure," Will said. He pocketed the envelope and stepped up to his saddle and rode out. And all the while he was remembering that just yesterday he'd heard the cook telling Blucher that in a couple of days someone must go to town for more supplies. What in hell made a letter so important that it couldn't wait another day or so? And why was William J. Yeoman always singled out for these little jaunts that made for an easy day's work?

He waited until a dip in the country put him out of sight of the ranch buildings before he looked at the letter and saw that it bore Carrico's name.

He'd long since ceased being surprised at the way the trails crossed and how near Fort Benton had come to stand to St. Louis. Frowning thoughtfully, he felt the envelope and found it thick but with no bulges to indicate the folds of a letter. He looked at the flap of the envelope and saw that it was sealed with wax. He turned the envelope over and studied the precise, scholarly fist of Brant Millard.

Something touched him then like a breath of wind — some feeling that he stood near to a truth as elusive as sunshine, as big as the horizons. Nothing he could get a hold on, just a feeling. It stirred deep in him. He carried that feeling across the miles to Fort Benton and knew what he would do when he got there.

He'd have liked to open the letter — this temptation was strong — but a better notion had struck him.

He rode in by way of the depot site and thought of the crowd that had gathered here not many days back. Now a couple of freight cars stood on a siding, and he saw that one was decorated with a huge canvas sign bearing the legend, "From P. H. Kelly Mercantile Company of St. Paul to I. G. Baker & Co. of Fort Benton. First car by rail to Fort Benton." This was somehow a lone, silent echo of the celebration. He rode over the brow of the hill, remembering the runaway, and so dropped down into Benton.

No brave bunting showing now, but only the tattered remnants of it hanging from some of the buildings. No teeming streets crowded with celebration-bound people. On Main he got a glimpse along one of the cross streets and saw a steamboat still at the levee. It looked as though the packet were being loaded for its downriver passage. He rode directly to the post office and turned in the letter.

Then he commenced his wait.

Long habit had made him careful of drawing unwonted attention to himself, so, after filching a piece of paper from a wastebasket, he moved to one of the counters and scratched away at a long, aimless letter to nobody. He was slow about this, spending as much time chewing at the end of the post office pen as he did at pretending to write.

After half an hour, he began to grow uneasy. It might be hours before Carrico would call for mail; in fact the man might not show up at all today. Was the postmaster beginning to wonder why a lone cowboy loitered so long? Will decided he would give himself another half hour and then saunter outside to watch for Carrico. He turned back to his make-believe letter, but all the while he was alert for footsteps; he heard the heavy, booted ones of men and the quick, lissome steps of women.

He listened to scraps of the talk of these townspeople. That freight car for I. G. Baker & Company held groceries, it seemed, and the other car was stocked with whiskey for the wholesale liquor department of Gans and Klein of Helena. Such had been Benton's first rail-borne freight. Something to eat, something to drink. Snow at Assiniboine, a man said, and a heavy fall of it in Helena. Might be a whopper of a winter, like the last one. Big talk at Great Falls about the celebration planned there for the coming of the Manitoba. "Well, we showed them how to do it," the postmaster observed.

Again Will wondered if he should move on

outside. Someone called for mail and expressed an opinion that that San Francisco fellow was really at work on an estimate for the iron bridge that was to be built across the Missouri. Looked like the ferry boat would soon be a thing of the past. Mighty big changes everywhere these days. Had the postmaster heard that sheep were going by rail from Big Sandy? Bootheels echoed across the room as this garrulous one departed and another entered.

Will heard the postmaster speak Carrico's name, and he turned and had his look.

He knew his risk full well. He was willing to run that risk. He'd had a glimpse of Carrico that night on the side street with Buck, seeing only a face he would have known anywhere. Now he saw that Carrico still wore black broadcloth and a show of jewelry and carried himself with that same fluid grace, but by daylight he was eight years older, and gray showed at his temples and sprinkled his inky mustache. Also, there was something awry about his nose. Will hadn't noticed that the other night. Then he remembered how Matt Comfort's fists had battered Carrico's face.

He stared at Carrico longer than he intended. He stared fascinated, feeling an odd sensation and recognizing it for the fear a boy had known. He told himself that the only danger from Carrico was a new danger but a greater one. Let Carrico recognize him and call his name, and he was fugitive again.

But Carrico was too absorbed to notice anyone's presence. Carrico had got only the one letter, and he'd at once turned his back on the postmaster's window and run a thumb under the flap. He drew forth the contents, a sheaf of bills. He counted these quickly and carefully; there were about ten, Will judged. Carrico thrust the bills back into the envelope and put it into his coat pocket and started for the door.

Will followed him as far as the doorway. Carrico was crossing the walk to climb into a waiting carriage. He spoke to someone within the carriage, but Will caught only a fragment of words. " . . . to the last penny . . . " Correct to the last penny? Carrico unwrapped the reins from the whip holder and wheeled the carriage completely around in the street, and thus Will got one quick glimpse of Zoe seated beside him.

Will shook his head. He'd wanted to see the contents of the envelope and, equally important, to witness Carrico's reaction to what the envelope had contained. Money. Brant Millard had mailed money to Carrico and had felt that the sending of that money was so important it must not be delayed even a day. But

175

what was the connection between the two men, and why was one paying money to the other? A gambling debt? Doubtless Carrico still worked at his old trade, and it was possible that Millard might have lost to him.

All of which was guesswork. Puzzled, Will walked to the hitchrail where he'd left his horse. Untying the reins, he stepped up into saddle. For a moment he had an impulse to follow Carrico's carriage, but he realized the futility of that; it would only lead him to wherever Carrico lived. Better not to risk crowding Carrico too closely and thus run the chance of being recognized. But still the questions plagued him. Frowning, he rode from town.

12

Cold Talk

With Fort Benton behind him, he chose at first to follow the river; and when he was not far out on the trail, he saw a rider and a pack horse ahead. A boy, he decided. The same instinct that had made him wary of drawing attention to himself in the post office now kept him a good distance behind the rider, but after a mile he realized that the pace of the one ahead was so slow that he, Will, would be long delayed. He'd spent much more time in Fort Benton than his mission had demanded, and he might have to explain his delay when he reported to Brant Millard. Wouldn't be seemly to be further delayed. Jogging his mount to greater speed, he overtook the rider and was almost past when he saw that she was Libbie Comfort.

He fell back stirrup to stirrup with her and said, "Good afternoon. I thought I recognized those braids when I got close."

"Oh, hello," she said. Her lips were thinned down. "I've got a firm hand on the reins today. There'll be no runaway for you to stop."

If she'd smiled as she'd spoken, he'd have construed her words to be nothing more than a reminder of their first meeting and therefore a bridge to friendliness. But there was truculence in her tone, that faint animosity he'd noticed at Diamond C. He wondered in what dark soil that animosity lay rooted. Buck Harper had called her nail-hard and said that she was a man-hater, yet there had been at the river ranch a glimpse of warmer moods. She interested him greatly. She was girl and woman and something else besides, something into which she had fashioned herself.

He glanced at the pack horse and noticed that its load was well balanced and the diamond hitch as neat as any. He wondered if this were her handiwork. He asked, "Supplies from town?"

"A crew on roundup seems to eat twice as much," she said.

He nodded. "Ours is about out of grub, too."

"I'm surprised," she said. "Hasn't Brant got an individual Dutch oven for each one of you and a bill of fare to choose from?"

"That reminds me," Will said. "I delivered

178

your message to him word for word. I don't think he was pleased. You've got it in for the man, haven't you?"

"No more than for any other man," she said.

He looked into her rebellious eyes and smiled. The sun had got at the tip of her nose and burned it, and the skin had peeled. Just the same, she had an attractive face, even in her stormier moods. There was a kind of beauty, like Zoe's, that struck a man sledge-hammer fashion; there was another kind that grew upon him the oftener he looked. Maybe Libbie's good looks came from within, not from any recognizable perfection of feature.

He asked, "What makes us men such a wicked lot?"

"Your insufferable arrogance," she said.

"You're thinking of Millard again. That doesn't go for all of us."

"Yes, it does," she said. "Deep inside, you think — every last one of you — that because you're men you throw a damn' big shadow."

Will had to grin. "Someone kissed you and ran away. That's it!"

He expected her to be angry, but she said in a matter-of-fact voice, "No man ever kissed me but my father. Just see how quickly you jumped to the wrong conclusion."

"Well," he said gravely. "I didn't have much to go on."

They rode in silence for several minutes; they rode with the river dreaming near at hand and the sky smiling and all the world smoky with autumn's haze. Against the hard-packed trail the hooves of the horses beat a steady rhythm.

At last Libbie spoke. "I was fourteen when my father died," she said. "He'd bought a piece of land and recorded a brand with the clerk of the Territorial supreme court. My father's dream was to raise cattle. My mother and I have tried to fulfill that dream. We raised our house mostly with our own hands. Later we got a crew. You've seen them. They look patched together with haywire, all except Buck. We've had to work right along with our crew. We've hauled water, and we've branded cattle, and we've sat a saddle straight as any man. Do you understand?"

Will nodded.

Her voice became heated. "And what has Brant Millard or any man had to say to that? Well done, my valiant ladies? No! We've done a man's work in a man's world, and the very fact has shocked everyone who's seen our efforts. Is the pride of men so fragile it can't stand any proof that a woman could equal them!"

Will said, "Some work is man's work."

She shook her head. "Now you're talking like Brant! He says he wants to marry me and give me the kind of life I deserve. His offering to loan men to help with the roundup was a typical gesture. But has he ever once told me that he's got a ranch to run, too, and that he needs me to help him run it? Has he ever acknowledged that I'd be of use other than to look pretty at the head of his table? Not that I've heard! I don't mean that I want to pound a saddle at B-M Connected. I'd be happy to live a woman's life for a change. But I'd like some damn' man to admit that I've proved I can do the same work he can."

He remembered her repulsing him when he'd offered to do his own unsaddling in Diamond C's barn. Now he understood. He said very solemnly, "Pay close attention. *I* say you've proved you can do a man's work."

For a moment he thought she was going to become angrier, and then she laughed. He liked the sound of her laughter.

"Do you know," she said, "you're good medicine."

He shrugged. "I was told in Benton that you've had rustler trouble."

At once her mood darkened again. "More than anyone else in our vicinity. You can see why. Night riders say to themselves that Diamond C is a petticoat layout and must be easy

181

pickings. But some night they're going to learn that a woman can shoot as straight as any man!"

Ahead of them the trail forked, one dim depression angling to the northwest across the grass. Libbie reined up. "You head that way," she said pointing. She looked at him and suddenly her face softened, and she was girlish and immature and altogether desirable. "I shouldn't have bothered you with all this talk," she said.

"I hope we'll do a lot more talking sometime," he said.

"Perhaps." She held her hand out to him. Then she nudged her horse along the branch of the trail that followed the river.

He watched her go, sitting his saddle as long as it took to spin up a cigarette. He got the tobacco fired, then headed along the other trail toward Millard's ranch. He felt strangely moved. In their other brief meetings, he had found her a stranger much more remote than the still tintype in Matt Comfort's watch, but today he'd come close to her for a few minutes and so begun to understand what had fashioned her into what she was. He remembered those chattering women in the Fort Benton store he and Buck had planned to rob; he remembered the expressed disgust of one because a woman had tried to wear a man's britches. He could see that Hagar Comfort and her daughter had battled more than storm and drought and the night-riding gentry; they had battled narrow-mindedness. He knew that Matt Comfort would have been proud of them.

He rode in a somber mood to B-M's ranch buildings.

He came upon them in late afternoon. From a low ridge, with ranch house and barn and bunkhouse spread below him, he saw a man step off the gallery, climb upon a ground-anchored horse and head toward the river at a leisurely gallop. That man was Buck Harper. At first he was surprised to find Buck here; then he supposed that Buck had come on some routine matter between the two ranches. Maybe some B-M strays had got into the Diamond C gather. He almost called to Buck before he realized the distance was too great. He guessed he bore Buck no ill will.

He had dismounted at the corrals when Millard came toward him from the house.

"The letter's posted," Will reported.

"It took you a time," Millard said, making it neither an accusation nor a reprimand.

Will had anticipated some such remark. "Had a shoe come loose just out of town," he said. "The horse started limping. It was easier to turn back to a blacksmith shop and have it fixed."

Millard nodded. He had a way of turning remote as though his flesh stood here in the empty yard but his spirit roamed far reaches. He said, "You might as well stay and sleep in the bunkhouse tonight. Most of the crew will be coming in. We've got the gather about finished, and it will only take a couple of the hands to hold it."

"Sure," Will said.

He found Henry Blucher in the bunkhouse, laying out a hand of solitaire. The two said nothing to each other. Within the hour the chuck-wagon came clattering into the yard, and better than half a dozen of the riders showed, too, whirling to the corrals and dismounting with a great jangling of spurs. Supper was late tonight, and darkness had fallen when the crew left the cook-shack to gather in the bunkhouse. Someone turned up a lamp, and the inevitable poker game got going.

Will found a magazine. He was thumbing the pages idly when Brant Millard framed himself in the doorway.

"Come on up to the house, Henry," Millard said. "I want to talk to you."

Blucher hadn't made a hand in the poker game but had turned again to the quirt he'd been so long at braiding. He looked up, his blue-stubbled face livening with interest. He put aside his work and left the bunkhouse at once. Will's own interest had quickened. At no other time had Millard ever had anything to say to Blucher that so pointedly couldn't be spoken before the crew. Will gave them ten minutes' start before he stretched himself, yawned widely, and strolled outside.

He made his way across the yard with studied slowness. Lamplight splashed from the cook-shack window; the coosie came to the doorway and emptied out a dishpan of water. He lifted his old face and stood listening to a trumpeting sky, his face eager and lonely. There was nobody else in sight. A breeze ran cool and gentle; overhead the wild geese cried, and Will looked up, too, but he couldn't see the dark wedge driving. It was full night now but not yet time for moonrise. Will quickened his pace, moving silently in the dark toward the house.

The only light burned in a big living room to the front of the building, and Will slipped off his boots before he came easing onto the gallery. Through the window he glimpsed bearskin rugs and fancy furniture; books were there and soft lamplight and a bright fire burning. Blucher sat slumped in a chair near the fireplace; Millard was talking intently, his hands moving and his face drawn tight.

There was too much of fall in the air for the window to be open, and only a faint murmur of sound reached Will. After a moment's debating, he catfooted to the door. He put his hand on the knob and took an eternity to push open the door. He hoped the slight draft would not make the living-room lamp flicker warningly. When the hinges squeaked, he paused, listening, but he heard only the thumping of his heart. He got into the dark hallway with doors giving off from it; a pencil of light showed under one of the doors.

Easing the outer door shut behind him, Will stood in a darkness so thick he felt he could touch it. Now he made out words clearly.

" . . . Sure you hate him," Millard was saying. "He made a pretty picture out of you with those fists of his. But believe me, you've got to keep that hate bottled up. Can't you see what I saw the minute he mentioned a job?"

Blucher's voice came rumbling. "Hell, you've been talking in circles, Brant. Tell me just one thing. How do you aim to fit him in?"

Me, Will thought and risked a step closer to the door.

"Look at the situation carefully, Henry. We've been giving the Comforts all the trouble possible, but still Mrs. Comfort won't sell out to me. And I'm convinced the girl isn't going to marry me to keep the ranch from going under, either. Still, I've kept playing the good neighbor. But this game can't go on forever."

"I don't see why not."

"Henry, what the Board of Stock Commissioners have done at other railroad points in the Territory they'll be doing along the Manitoba. Stock inspectors at all shipping centers. Shippers expected to show a receipt of purchase for any stock not bearing their brand. There'll be inspectors at St. Paul and Chicago, too. It's going to mean the end of rustling, my friend. But what's more to the point, even a blind man can see that the outfit most in need of that Diamond C river acreage is mine."

"Nobody's raised a voice against you yet."

"No, but other ranchers are getting aroused over the rustling, even though it's only hit hard at Diamond C. Clark and another of those fellows from up north spoke to me about it in town not long ago. One of these days some busybody will start cutting for long-looping sign, and there'll be nothing to show the work of outsiders. Then they'll really begin to wonder who's behind it all, and it won't take them long to figure out who stands to gain. The fact that I'm courting the girl won't throw any dust in their eyes. I'm too old for her. Any blind man can see that, too."

"But how does that fist-slinging squirt — ?"

"How does he fit in? Perfectly — when the time comes. That's why he's got to be treated gently meanwhile. Remember that first morning he was here — the morning I rode out and put you and the boys to working over those Diamond C steers till their brands looked like something from the other side of the Judith? I had our friend on a wild-goose chase, carrying a message to the Comforts. Today I gave him another soft job, mailing money to that damn' Carrico. I've kept him out of the way, and I've made it a soft berth for him. That's why I've kept telling you to go easier on him. We want him sticking around till we need him."

"And when will that be?"

"Soon, Henry." Millard's voice lowered. He sounded to Will like a man with a talent for conspiracy and a great enjoyment in it. "Diamond C has obligingly rounded up all their gather. One of these nights we'll run it off. Over the bluffs and into the river."

"You don't aim to blot the brands and sell the stuff?"

"Why bother? One last stroke, and Hagar Comfort is bankrupt. But first we'll fire one of her haystacks. Tonight, Henry. Noonan should be a good man for that job. Unless I miss my guess, Mrs. Comfort won't leave any more than two of her pensioners holding the herd after that. The others will be keeping an

188

eye on the haystacks the next few nights."

Blucher's voice rose excitedly. "And that's when we'll hit at the herd!"

"Exactly. But after the raid, there'll be a dead rustler to show — a rustler those good neighbors, the B-M boys, nailed. Our friend Slim. Sure, he worked for us. But there was something shady about him — he wouldn't give his name. Remember, Henry? Must be he was an inside man for the rustlers. When some of our boys, riding home from town of a night, saw the Diamond C herd being shoved along by strangers, they opened fire. And there was Slim. Too bad the rest got away, the cattle with them."

"I savvy," Blucher said with great satisfaction. "I surely do. One dead stranger who'll make it look like outsiders were operating on this range all along. And no finger pointed at us, since we'll be producing the carcass. One dead stranger! Brant, that chore is sure as hell mine!"

"The whole chore is yours," Millard said. "You can start by calling Noonan out of the bunkhouse and putting him on that haystack job. I'll leave it to you to decide which night will be best to hit their herd. I'll likely be on my way downriver by then. If that packet is going to get out of Benton before a freeze, it should be leaving any time. The captain promised he'd send me word. Either I'm on it, or I'll have to wait till spring. You're the big boss till I get back, Henry. Have you got everything straight?"

"Straight enough."

Silence fell, and Will wondered if he shouldn't get out of here. Then Millard spoke again.

"One more thing," Millard said. "I'll take the wagon and head straight to the river, once word comes that the packet has got up steam. No point in boarding at Benton. I can hail the boat from that old landing Diamond C uses when they have freight put ashore. You can either drive me down or else send one of the boys after the wagon and team. Meanwhile you'd better get the wagon loaded."

"I'll get at that right away, Brant."

A chair scuffed against the floor as Blucher came to a stand. Will glided to the outer door and got his hand on the knob. Blucher's voice rumbled again, and under cover of that sound, Will got through the doorway and out upon the gallery. A moment later he was picking up his boots and fading around a corner of the house.

Now he was done with waiting; in all his chaotic thinking as he stomped into his boots that was the one thing that stood clear. He knew where he must go and for what purpose, and his trail would lead straight to Diamond C. He looked over his shoulder, and the stocky shape of Blucher loomed out of the darkness.

Will moved to the yard pump and worked its handle lustily. He had the water dipper raised to his lips when Blucher's voice cut through the night, calling out to him.

13

Clash by Night

There was in Will only a flicker of fear that Blucher might have known of his eaves-dropping and so was calling him to account. If Blucher had known, then Blucher's gun would have spoken out of the darkness, not his voice. Therefore Will quelled his first instinctive alarm and finished having his drink of water, sloshing what was left upon the ground. He turned toward Blucher and said, "Yes — ?" Impatience built in him, a driving desire to be up into saddle and on his way to Diamond C. His real fear was that Blucher had some chore that might hold him here. Stay then he must, or show his hand by riding out.

Blucher moved closer and grunted his recognition. "Come along and earn your wages," he said.

"Sure," Will said. Silently he followed as Blucher led the way across the yard to a small shed that was padlocked. Will was still stunned by what he'd overheard between Blucher and Millard. That B-M was indeed behind the rustling was surprise enough; that the rustling had been calculated to drive the Comforts off their land made little sense, even though he, Will, had once suspected as much. But that had been before he'd known B-M. Why did Millard, who gave no real attention to his own acreage, want more?

Blucher, fumbling with a key, had got the shed open, and the two of them stepped into a dark interior, rancid with the leathery smell of saddles and harness. Dust was here, too, and cobwebs. Blucher moved about; Will stood still, not knowing the way.

"Here," Blucher finally said. "Get hold of one end of this box. Feel it? We're moving it to the wagon shed."

The box was heavy, but easy enough for two men to handle; and when they got outside where Will could see its outline, he judged that it was something like the rough box for a coffin, only bulkier. They toted it to the wagon shed and slid it into the bed of a light spring wagon, and Blucher said, "That's all, feller."

Nodding, Will strolled away, trying not to appear in a hurry. Queer how tight his stomach felt, as though he'd eaten something that disagreed with him.

He got to the corral where he'd put his bay, and here he paused, forcing himself to take time to shape up a cigarette. After he got the smoke going, he had a quick look around and did some sharp listening. Blucher was moving about somewhere in the yard. Cook-shack and bunkhouse still glowed with light; the ranch house stood dark on the side nearest Will. He dropped the cigarette to the ground and put his boot upon it.

Snaking out his horse, he got gear onto the bay and led the mount toward the bunkhouse. He dropped the reins and stepped inside. The eternal poker game was still in progress and tobacco smoke layered the air. Those not involved with cards lolled about or rested in the bunks.

Will asked casually, "Anybody like to ride into town with me?"

He was gambling that none would volunteer. No one spoke up in direct answer; but one, Noonan, said, "We'll be moving our beef to town soon. Can't your thirst keep till then?" He was a stringy man, this Noonan, with the sharp face of a ferret.

An older hand laughed. "Slim's a young 'un. It's the girls he's missing, not the whiskey."

Noonan said, "Better be here at the crack of

sunrise. Henry will have your hide if you show up late."

"I'll be back early," Will said.

Thus he fixed it so his departure wouldn't arouse instant suspicion. This done, he stepped up into saddle, lifted the bay to a brisk trot and headed out of the yard. When he looked over his shoulder, the bunkhouse doorway was showing a rectangle of light as Blucher entered. Will whistled softly.

Once the night had closed around him, he circled the ranch buildings and lined out for the river. He brought the bay to a gallop; the dark earth drummed beneath him, the breeze of his own making sharp against his face. Faint stars began to show, and a slice of moon stood on the eastern horizon. He rode as swiftly as the way permitted, but sometimes he drew to a halt, swung about in his saddle and listened hard. Once he dismounted and put an ear to the ground. Somewhere behind him Noonan would be coming.

Noonan was his immediate concern. That Millard had business downriver and was taking some ponderous crate along was nothing to excite Will. That Millard had first set into motion machinery designed to strike one last, ruinous blow at Diamond C was quite another matter. First the burned haystack — later the full-scale raid. Stop the one, and he might give pause to the other.

This was all the plan he had as he came toward the Comfort ranch. Into the river breaks, he had to slow his pace; the land lay formless by night, a bulking of dim rises, a lake of uncertain shadows; and he was not sure of his way. He grew panicky thinking he might have aimed too far north or south, and then, distantly, he heard a dog bark. He hadn't remembered seeing a dog at Diamond C, but he oriented the sound and headed toward it and so came to a hogback ridge that topped the draw leading to the ranch buildings.

Below he saw a dim fire burning and made out a mass of cattle. The river-ranch gather. He skirted the roundup camp by staying on the ridge until he was above the ranch buildings. Here he found the trail that had brought Diamond C's crew down that day he'd eaten dinner here. Getting toward midnight, he judged; but light glowed in the house as he rode up, and the dog came to meet him, barking and leaping.

By the time he'd stepped down from saddle, the door was open and Libbie stood silhouetted against the light.

Will said incongruously, "I didn't know you had a dog."

Libbie peered. "Oh, it's you!" A measure

of relief softened her tone. "Shep, come in here! Shep was sleeping in the barn the day you were here."

From somewhere in the house, Mrs. Comfort called, "Who is it, Elizabeth?"

"Slim, from B-M Connected, Mother." To Will she said, "Come in, won't you?"

He pulled off his hat and was ushered into the living room.

Hagar Comfort sat in a rocking chair, a pair of spectacles upon her nose, a book open in her lap. The dog had curled up by her chair. Mrs. Comfort looked up, smiling; she extended her hand. "I'm so sorry I wasn't home when you called before. I'm glad you've come again. Elizabeth, get a chair for him."

He made an impatient gesture. He had no time for small talk, and the question in him was how he would tell them what they must know. "Have you any close neighbors who could come and help you?" he asked. "Outside of Brant Millard, I mean." It was a clumsy beginning, he knew.

Mrs. Comfort frowned in bewilderment. "What do you mean?"

He sensed Libbie's still presence at his elbow; Libbie, too, was waiting. He wanted to blurt out all of it — who he was and what had really happened on the *Cherokee* long, long ago, and why he was here now. He wanted to lay the whole truth before them, and he couldn't, and that was what made it so difficult to sort out the one fragment he could now offer.

He said desperately, "I know you're in trouble. That notice you had in the Benton paper, looking for friends of your husband. I saw it."

"Trouble with rustlers," Hagar Comfort admitted. "My husband helped many people in his lifetime; it hasn't been too hard on my pride to ask his old friends to come and help me. But they're scattered now, and it will take time for many of them to get here. I've had letters from all over — wonderful letters. Tell me, young man, were you a friend of my husband?"

Again Will made an impatient gesture. "You know that I work for Millard," he said. "You've got to believe what I tell you. Tonight I heard him talking to his foreman. Millard is behind the trouble you've been having. Right now one of his men is riding here to set a haystack afire. That's a trick to have you watching your other stacks the next few nights. And while you're busy guarding them, B-M will strike at your cattle."

Beside him, Libbie drew in a sharp breath.

Mrs. Comfort let the book slip from her lap to the floor. She looked as though she'd been slapped. She said, "You must be mistaken!"

"But I'm not!"

"But Mr. Millard has been so neighborly through all our trouble — time and again he's offered me loans to buy more stock." She shook her head. She was, Will judged, a woman without guile, who therefore found it hard to see guile in another. She looked up at Will. "Why, he's even spoken for Elizabeth's hand."

"He wants the river acreage," Will said. "He'll marry Libbie to get it, if necessary. But it's the land he's really after. The man's a considerable fool."

Libbie said, "That's the most roundabout compliment I've ever received!"

Mrs. Comfort shook her head again. "Brant Millard! I just can't believe it!"

Will said, "And while we're talking about it, a B-M rider may be out there firing a haystack!"

Libbie moved into Will's range of vision. She crossed over to a rack that held several garments. From a peg she picked a buckskin jacket and shrugged into it; then she took a belt with holster and gun from another peg and flung the belt around her middle and latched it. "There's a good way to test the truth of all this," she announced. "I'm going out to the haystacks."

Will said sharply, "It's not safe!"

She looked fierce and angry. "Damn it, don't you yet believe that I can hold a man's place!"

Will said, "I'm coming with you."

"Then come along." She crossed quickly to her mother. "Now don't you worry," she said. "If there's a man out there, he's going to get a surprise. If there isn't, this one's going to have to do some tall explaining." She flung herself to the door and pulled it open.

Will gave Mrs. Comfort a quick glance. "Everything will be all right," he promised, and followed Libbie out.

She said, "Your horse can stand where it is. Better to walk to the haystacks." She struck out in the direction of the river, and he hurried after her; she strode briskly for perhaps a quarter of a mile. The draw widened out to become a bottom-land meadow along the river. Here the haystacks loomed up; moonlight glinted on the barbed wire strung around them to keep stray stock from the fodder. There were no more than half a dozen of these stacks. Libbie paused in the shadow of one.

"This is as good a place to wait as any," she said. She whispered it.

He squatted down on his heels. He wanted mightily to smoke, but he didn't dare show a light. He wanted to talk, but he knew the need for silence. A wind moved off the river; it was a cold wind. The moon had climbed high, but the heavens were cloud wracked, and darkness lay often on the land.

When light showed, he studied Libbie's face. It was inflexible, strong with determination. It crossed his mind that he'd never seen her wearing a dress. The minutes dragged leaden feet, and small worries began to beset him. Had Blucher been alarmed by his leaving the ranch, even though he, Will, had made a to-do to give the impression that he was going to town? Had Brant Millard, with his genius for conspiracy, decided on a new plan? These questions crowded at him.

Then Libbie stiffened. "Listen!" she whispered.

He heard the strike of hoofs. The sound seemed to come from everywhere and nowhere. He strained his eyes and at last made out the vague form of a horse and rider no more than a hundred yards away. Will came to a stand and moved close to Libbie and suddenly realized she was trembling. He put an arm around her and held her close. She stood stiff and motionless within the circle of his arm. He said very quietly, "Easy! Easy!"

The horseman drew closer, reining up by the first of the haystacks and dismounting. He fumbled at the makeshift gate in the wire. He became lost in the shadow of the stack, and then the flame of a match showed. The man had paper wadded in his hand. He lighted the paper and thrust this improvised torch against the haystack. There had been enough rain and snow lately so that the hay did not at once catch. Libbie made a movement to break free of Will.

"Stay here!" he whispered fiercely.

He released her and knelt and slipped off his spurs. He glided forward, coming toward B-M's man at an oblique angle. He lifted his gun from its holster and sprinted the last few yards to the opening in the wire. Darting inside, he laid the barrel of the gun across the crown of the man's wide hat. The man groaned and fell into a heap, the torch dropping from his hand. Instantly Will tromped on the paper, extinguishing the blaze.

Libbie came running up. Will scraped a match aglow and bent and rolled the man over and held the light close to his face. The man was quite unconscious. Will took the man's gun and hurled it far away.

"Noonan!" Libbie breathed.

Will stood up. "What will we do with him?"

Libbie didn't answer. Instead she placed her hands on Will's shoulders and looked him in the face. Her expression had turned soft. "For whatever moment's doubt I had of you in the house, I apologize."

He said, "You never really had any doubt. Otherwise you wouldn't have trusted me to come out here with you."

Her lips trembled. She had not been so shaken as this the day of the runaway. "We've had trouble before, but this is different from a morning's report of how many cattle turned up missing. When he rode up — " She began to tremble again.

He said quickly, "It's over now." He glanced toward the fallen man and asked again, "What will we do with him?"

"I wonder," she said. "I could have our crew take him to Benton and lodge him in the jail."

He shook his head. He was remembering Millard's talent for conspiracy. "B-M would probably claim they'd just fired him. Millard could even prove neighborliness by all this. Noonan, sore at B-M for being let go, hadn't dared to hit at Millard. So, to get even, he'd set out to make trouble for Millard's good friends, the Comforts. Do you see how it could be made to look? For fifty dollars, Noonan could be bought to back up such a story."

"I suppose," she said.

Inspired, he walked to Noonan's ground-anchored horse. He picked up the reins and knotted them at the saddle horn, then slapped the horse across the rump with his hat and sent the mount galloping into the night.

"Let's leave Noonan where he is," he said. "When he wakes up and finds himself afoot, he won't risk trying to fire any haystack. He couldn't get away without your crew's running him down. He'll hotfoot it back to B-M. And that outfit will have a scare thrown into them."

She said, "You think it's safe?"

"Put yourself in Noonan's boots." He looked off into the night. "Have you got any near neighbor who would lend you help?"

"There's Clark, up north along the river. His outfit is small, but his crew combined with ours would make around a dozen."

He got his spurs and buckled them on. He took her arm and started back toward the house. He was silent for a while, thinking hard. "Get word to Clark right away," he said. "Ask him to spare as many men as he can. His boys and yours can watch over your gather until the beef is aboard railroad cars. If B-M is bold enough to strike meanwhile, you'll be able to give them a surprise."

"Better to go to Clark, you think, than to talk to the law at Benton?"

Will nodded. "You can't expect deputies to sit out here night after night just on suspicion. And if they do come, the word will likely get around and B-M will lay off. Better that they should strike and be caught at it, so this business can be ended once and for all. There's a chance they may be scared off anyway, once Noonan reports. But" — he was remembering that Millard would be gone and Blucher in charge — "I don't think so."

They had reached the walk leading to the house. Will's horse stood waiting. "And what about you?" Libbie asked.

"Do you keep any whiskey for medicine?"

"A little," she said, puzzled.

"Give me some to take along," he said. "I'm going back to B-M. They think I've ridden to town. I want to come in with whiskey on my breath and the smell of it on my clothes. My scheme is to ride with that crew a little longer. Don't you see? It may be that I'll know when they're ready to strike."

"I'll get the whiskey," she said. She stepped into the house, leaving the door open behind her. He could hear her speak to her mother reassuringly, but he didn't follow after her. Libbie could do the explaining to Hagar Comfort. He'd have to be on his way to B-M soon, if he were ever going back. Libbie came to the doorway again and handed him a pint bottle. He stood in the splash of light and she regarded him gravely. She was a warm presence now, liking him, grateful to him.

"Why are you doing this for us?" she asked.

He had no answer. He had found her to be a brave one tonight for all her trembling and the need for his arm. Brave enough to go into the night and the danger. He was immeasurably closer to her for what had happened this last hour but not yet so close he could speak the truth. He only shook his head. "I must be riding," he said.

"Ride well and safely." She closed the door.

He picked up the reins of the bay and walked over to the horse trough and let the bay have a drink. He tightened the cinch and set his foot to the stirrup and felt the grind of a gun at his back. His sickening thought was *Noonan!* and he half turned, surprised, not expecting this of Noonan, not expecting boldness. Then he remembered how far he had hurled Noonan's gun and how soundly he had left Noonan sleeping.

The gun at his back cocked, and that warning click stopped him. He heard his name spoken. All of time dissolved then, the rawhide years running a full circle back to their beginning; for the voice belonged to Marshal Sam Littlejohn.

14

The Law's Wide Loop

This first wild moment held only the sudden breath of surprise, and then, with the full truth striking him, it seemed not strange to Will that Littlejohn had at last caught up with him. The man had been born to pursue him, and Littlejohn had crowded his heels across the years and the miles and through the tangled threads of Will's dreaming. Because of Littlejohn he had chosen the wilderness that night long ago. Because of Littlejohn he had avoided Fort Benton for eight years. Always the marshal had been on the edge of his consciousness; always Will had been wary, expecting the cocked gun, the familiar voice. And always he had feared there would be this meeting. Now it had happened.

Littlejohn's voice was harsh with anger. "To have found you *here*, of all places! By

God, haven't you done enough to these people?" He lifted the gun from Will's holster. He moved his free hand over Will and found the whiskey bottle Will had stowed inside his shirt. It might have made a club; Littlejohn hurled it away. "Up on your horse, you," Littlejohn ordered.

Will said, quietly desperate, "Just take me into the house first and talk to the Comforts about why I'm here. Ten minutes will do it."

Littlejohn said flatly, "I'm doing no damn' favor for you."

"But it's for them!"

"Up on your horse," Littlejohn ordered again. "I'll give you no chance to get a woman's skirts between you and my gun. Or whatever other trick you've got in mind."

Here was the old stubbornness of mind Will had known on the St. Louis levee and in the darkness of Dakota. He could lay hold of no weapon to pit against that stubbornness. Soon Libbie would be on her way to get Clark's help. Soon the combined crews of Diamond C and the neighboring ranch would be laying a trap around the precious Comfort herd. His job was to get back to B-M and so be able to spy on Millard's crew, to know the hour when they would strike. This was his great need, but where was the chance when Littlejohn stood so unyielding?

Will mounted. Littlejohn's stocky form moved away in the darkness, and Will thought, *Now — ?* but remembered Littlejohn's gun. The marshal loomed up astride a horse. He said, "Ahead of me," and made a motion. They went riding up the south slant of the draw and cut for the river, flanking the haystacks by a good distance.

Will was remembering Lem Singleton who hadn't recognized him, and Zoe who'd looked so long by lamplight after he'd asked, "Zoe, don't you know me?" He said to Littlejohn bitterly, "So you never forget a face."

"Not in my business," Littlejohn said. "I studied you standing in the light of the doorway. At first you seemed only slightly familiar. You've changed, but you're Will Yeoman."

Will asked, "How long have you been a step behind me?"

They had begun to parallel the river; they moved south toward Benton. This was a wide trail they followed, and Will judged it to be the one over which Libbie had come with the pack horse and supplies after leaving him at the fork to B-M. Littlejohn rode half a horse behind him; but Will by turning his head, could see the marshal. The man wore the garb of a working cowboy, but his thousand-year-old face was the same, blank and weary, and the heavy mustache looked as black as ever. Littlejohn shook his head.

"I've met irony before," he said. "Time and again I've cut sign on a wanted man only to turn up a little late on his trail. Then, when I'm least expecting to, I walk right into someone like you. My work brought me overland to Benton today. I've never come to this section without taking time to visit Mrs. Comfort, but tonight I came especially because a notice in the *River Press* was called to my attention. She was asking help from her husband's old friends. The last person in the world I expected to find at her place was you."

Irony! More than the marshal knew, Will observed. It was the same newspaper notice that had fetched both of them. He asked, "What was Matt Comfort to you?"

At first Littlejohn didn't answer. Then he said, "Matt Comfort? A man with a musket in his hand, standing beside me at Pittsburg Landing. A man who carried me on his back to where the doctors were lopping off shattered arms and legs, then stood by to make sure they sewed me up instead of amputating. I don't even limp when I walk, you may have noticed."

Will said, "Since Matt meant so much to you, I'm asking you to listen to what brought me to Diamond C."

"I listen to any man," Littlejohn said. His voice turned harsh again. "I do not think I'll believe anything you tell me. I've tried to keep impersonal about the men I've had to hunt. But I've told you what Matt Comfort meant to me. Now you understand why I hate you right down to the ground, Yeoman."

Will said, "I saw that newspaper notice, too." He told it all then — why he'd chosen to work for B-M and how patience had brought him outside Brant Millard's door tonight. He ended by telling of the encounter with Noonan at the haystack and his talk with Libbie afterward and the plan they'd laid. "Don't you see," he added, "that I've got to get back to B-M?"

Littlejohn shook his head. "I'm taking you to the Benton jail."

"But if you'll take me back to Diamond C, Libbie and her mother will back my story!"

Littlejohn said, "And what if there is a half-truth behind it? Where's the proof that you haven't betrayed this Millard for your own gain? I'm remembering how you turned against Carrico for Matt's sake and then turned on Matt. What do you intend to get out of Hagar Comfort? You have nothing in your record to make me trust you."

Futility rose in Will, a sense of battering

against a wall; but temper tugged at him, too. "Have you ever in your life been wrong and faced up to it?"

Littlejohn said, "I treat each thing in its proper time and in the order of its importance. If the Comforts need help, they'll have mine — when I'm free to give it."

"But you'll be too damn' late!"

"There is a more important matter, as Hagar Comfort would be the first to agree. I want you under lock and key. How can I believe you're a friend of the Comforts when I know there's blood on your hands? So first I'm going to sweat a name out of you — the name of the man who hired you to sink a knife into Matt Comfort."

Will fought hard to hold to patience. He said, "I heard you ask for a horse in Dakota; I was there that night you spoke to the crowd at the landing. You said I was the only passenger who couldn't be accounted for and that none of the yawls was missing. Tell me, Littlejohn, how did it strike you that the wooden Indian had been taken? Didn't that shake your notion that Matt's death was a simple business of a kid's killing him for his money?"

Littlejohn said, "What kind of dust are you trying to throw in my eyes now? Sure, the missing Indian gave me a new notion, but it didn't clear you. I didn't know about the Indian that night. You see, the captain was up and about and thought he heard a commotion on the boiler deck. When he went to investigate, he found the door of Matt's cabin open. His sense of alarm took him inside, and he found Matt dead. The captain came at once to my cabin. I only glanced in Matt's cabin and then started searching the boat for you. You were missing. I left the boat that night, as you seem to know."

"I found Matt dead before the captain found him," Will interjected. "I was too excited to notice that the Indian was gone."

"I'll bet you were," Littlejohn said scathingly. "I learned the significance of the Indian later, when I got a report from my men in St. Louis. I wrote to the captain. He told me the Indian had vanished the night of the murder. It was all clear to me then. By prearrangement someone overtook the *Cherokee* with a yawl. You went overboard into that yawl, and the Indian went with you."

"All right, Littlejohn," Will said wearily. "Then what about the Indian? What made it so valuable?"

They were still skirting the river; a breeze moved across the river and reached through Will's clothes. The moon scurried in and out of the cloud wrack, sometimes hidden, sometimes dappling the face of the water. Around

213

them bluffs lifted and great shadows grew. Through the night Littlejohn rode long in silence.

"You think I've never faced up to a mistake," he said at last. "In my business no man could survive who did not keep remembering how easy it is to make a mistake. I think I'll tell you a few things, Yeoman. The knowledge won't hurt you, and it certainly won't go beyond you, for I shall keep you locked up till all the truth is out."

"I'm listening," Will said, but no hope grew in him. This was like poker, he judged; Littlejohn was playing the cards he held and bluffing in the hope of seeing his opponent's hand.

"About ten years ago, when the river trade was flourishing, a gang of wreckers started working between here and St. Louis. Sometimes they scuttled steamers and burned them after removing everything of value; sometimes they took what they wanted at gunpoint and rode off laughing. They terrorized the river. Because mail and government cargo were often involved, I and other marshals were assigned at St. Louis to run them down."

Will's interest quickened. "I heard a lot of talk at Carrico's bar about river-wreckers."

"So did I," Littlejohn said. "The rank and file are frontier renegades. The higher-ups are sharp men. Oh, we learned a great deal about them; one of our men even worked with them for a while. He was later found near Omaha floating with a knife in his back. But such reports as he managed to get through had been meaty. The rank and file were paid off with the bulkier loot — trade goods that had been intended for Benton stores, buffalo robes consigned to St. Louis. The higher-ups took the most valuable stuff — gold dust, minted money, jewels that had been stored in captains' safes by lady passengers. And that kind of loot always came eventually to their St. Louis headquarters, where they kept it hid."

"Must have made quite a treasure."

"Exactly. A mighty bulky treasure. So eventually they swapped the dust and money for jewels, too, and that way the loot got converted into a mere handful of jewels, mostly diamonds. And they ended up in a cleverly contrived wooden cigar-store Indian that was hollow and had a removable head."

Will started.

"Ah, that means something to you," Littlejohn said. "Yes, it was the same Indian Matt Comfort was taking up to Benton. Only Matt, of course, didn't know he was hauling a king's ransom inside the thing. Nor did I, at the time."

"But how did Matt come by that particular Indian?"

"In '79 my men were all ready to close in on the St. Louis headquarters of the wrecking gang — a little tobacco shop in the riverfront section. But there was a leak, somehow. The wreckers knew we were hot on their trail, so they were mighty anxious to get that loot moved. But how to do it? Their own men might be marked and watched by the law, for all they knew. They had to have a stranger move the loot out of St. Louis for them. And along came big Matt Comfort from Montana Territory, looking for a wooden Indian for his little girl."

"You mean that's how they got the idea of fixing up a wooden Indian as a cache?"

"Obviously," Littlejohn said. "Somebody suggested to Matt the right place to buy a wooden Indian, then hurried to have the Indian prepared and waiting. That someone is high up in the wrecking gang, possibly at the very top. But Matt's dead, so identification of the man is impossible."

"Wait!" Will said, and he was reaching deep into memory. "Matt spoke about that. I asked him how he'd located the big chief. He said he'd met a Montana man and told him about wanting a wooden Indian. In fact, he met the man at Carrico's."

Excitement edged Littlejohn's voice. "And who was that man? You were there. Do you remember Matt's talking to anyone at Carrico's?"

Will shook his head. "Matt came to the place four nights running. It must have been one of the first nights that he got put on the trail of the Indian, because he had the big chief aboard the packet that last night. Matt was a friendly man. He bought drinks left and right and talked to anyone who would listen. Several men sat in at the poker games with him each night, too. There were too many faces. I just don't remember."

Littlejohn said, "More dust in my eyes, eh?"

"Damn it," Will said, "if I could remember, I'd tell you!"

"The man who talked to Matt is one I've been after for ten years," Littlejohn said. "That's why I was aboard the *Cherokee* that run. While my deputies were getting set to close in on the tobacco shop, I was riding the river to see that none of the wreckers who were known to us were slipping out of St. Louis. The raid on the tobacco shop was made the same morning the *Cherokee* was set to steam out."

"And you saw nobody aboard the packet?"

Littlejohn had drawn up stirrup to stirrup with Will. He sat deep in his saddle, a stocky man with a face turned thoughtful. Was the beginning of doubt in him, Will wondered, the first crack in that wall of stubbornness?

"Nobody I was looking for," Littlejohn said. "Luck went against us. The raid bagged only a few underlings. One talked. He told about that Indian, but the report didn't reach me till I got to Fort Benton weeks later. Then I realized it must have been the very Indian Matt was toting, and the captain's letter confirmed that the Indian had disappeared the night Matt was murdered. That's when I shaped up a new notion about you. I decided you'd been put aboard by the wreckers to get that Indian overboard before the boat reached Benton. A lot of rogues hung out around Carrico's. One of them could have hired you."

"Somebody did come aboard in Dakota to get the Indian," Will said. "It would have been too risky to make a play for the loot at Fort Benton, I suppose. A man killed Matt, then lowered the Indian to friends who were keeping abreast of the packet with a yawl. I fought that man, Littlejohn. That must have been the commotion the captain heard. The two of us tumbled overboard. I swam ashore, then walked to that Dakota settlement. I heard what you said about me before you began your hunt. I've been running from you ever since."

Littlejohn drummed with his fingertips

upon his saddle horn. "Are you talking straight? Still, there's no proof a man came aboard. Maybe only one went overboard. *You.*"

Will said, "I can't give you any proof. I know that."

Littlejohn said thoughtfully, "I've got to be careful. The game is shaping up for its finish now. We've played our cards close ever since we failed on that St. Louis raid. To all appearances we've laid off that wrecking gang, but actually we've watched them closer than they know. They've got another rendezvous in St. Louis, and they've piled up even more loot. But we've got another of our men working on the inside. He tells us the gang is ready to break and scatter. They know that with the railroads into Montana, the day of the riverboat is done. But first they'll have to divide their loot. When they get together to do that, we'll have all our birds in one nest. We'll close in on them then."

"Then the job is as good as done," Will said. "Why can't you go back to Diamond C? Your gun can help if B-M strikes. Take me with you, or let me go to B-M."

Littlejohn said, "I've already told you: There's no proof that you're not tied in with that wrecking crew. If you get a chance to slip away, you could send word to St. Louis and scatter the rest of them like prairie chickens in the brush."

Will shook his head. He had made his plea, and it had been something hurled against a wall to lie broken. He rode on in silence, busy at thinking; he shaped words to make new appeals to Littlejohn but left them unspoken, realizing their uselessness. He held to silence until Fort Benton loomed up ahead. The night was nearly gone; only a few lights still twinkled on Front Street.

They came in by way of the fort; and in the shadow of that gray adobe wall, Will drew rein. Instantly Littlejohn was crowding close to him, and Will guessed that the gun had come into Littlejohn's hand.

Will said desperately, "Go back to Diamond C, Littlejohn. That's all I ask. Lock me up, but go back and help them."

Littlejohn loomed close to him in the murk. The marshal said, "You talked about a man and his mistakes. Matt Comfort was my friend. Because of that, I once left my job and took your trail when my real duty lay elsewhere. If I'd stayed aboard the *Cherokee*, I'd have discovered that the Indian was gone, and I might have jumped at the truth sooner than I did. In any case, I'd have got here to Benton sooner and got my report from St. Louis. Maybe this job has been eight years longer because I forgot where my duty lay."

"But you went out to Diamond C tonight because of Mrs. Comfort's notice in the paper. You told me so. You meant to help her."

"I meant to ask her about her troubles, Yeoman. Then, if the time came when I could lend a hand, I'd know what I was doing. But I know that Hagar Comfort would tell me that finishing a ten year job of rounding up a crew of river renegades is more important than what may be happening to her herd one of these nights. Especially when the gang I'm after includes the man who made a widow of her. My job here is to cut sign on the Montana end of the river gang."

"That's your final answer?"

"Final," Littlejohn said.

Will drew in his breath sharply as a thought struck him. What Littlejohn had told him tonight, tied to his own jumbled thinking on these last silent miles of the trail, had prompted a sudden suspicion. What about that box Henry Blucher and he had loaded into a wagon for Brant Millard? He remembered the weight of the box and the shape of it, and he saw the dim outline of a startling truth. There were things that fitted and things that didn't, but the full answer might be reached.

His first reaction was to lay his notion before Littlejohn and perhaps smash through the wall of Littlejohn's stubbornness. He instantly chose not to. Littlejohn put no trust in him, thinking Will Yeoman to be devious and blood-guilty. Littlejohn might think this a new ruse and so take no action until it was too late. Let the last steamboat go, and the box was gone — and the chance. Whatever must be done must be of Will's doing.

Littlejohn had taken his gun, but he'd left him his spurs. He jabbed those spurs hard into the flanks of the bay and at the same time hauled on the reins, lifting the horse to a rearing stand. He neck-reined the bay hard against Littlejohn's horse. The marshal's gun exploded, the flame blinding Will, but he'd thrown Littlejohn off aim. He struck out at Littlejohn, the blow lifting Littlejohn from his saddle.

Bending low, Will spurred the bay again, bringing the horse to a gallop. He cut through the darkness here by the fort; he heard Littlejohn's wild shout and the bark of Littlejohn's gun. The man was shooting blindly, Will knew, but the bay broke stride and stumbled, and Will kicked free of the stirrups. He lighted on his shoulder and went rolling. His mouth was brassy with the taste of defeat.

15

Fugitive

He came up running. He wasn't sure whether his horse was wounded; he only knew that the bay was down. He liked that horse, and anger touched him that the horse might have got hurt. He sprinted off into the darkness; looking back over his shoulder, he saw the flash of Littlejohn's gun. The marshal's horse seemed to be rearing, and Will wondered if Littlejohn were trying to shoot and snatch at the reins at the same time. He saw his own mount struggling to get up.

This frantic minute, Will knew, might be his only margin. He ran on, pounding as hard as he could; he ran in a zig-zag fashion as Littlejohn's gun beat again and again. He had to get to cover before Littlejohn was back into saddle.

From Front, he crossed over on the first side street and reached Main. Only a few wayfarers were abroad at this hour, but Will knew that the beat of Littlejohn's gun must have alerted them, so he dropped to a walk. It was hard holding to this pace; every instinct screamed that he run.

He saw a man coming toward him, and he adopted the shambling, lurching walk of a drunk. The man peered at Will and asked, "What the hell's going on?" Will stumbled toward the nearest building and put his hand to the wall and made a retching noise deep in his throat. The man muttered something and moved on.

Will listened and was sure hoofs were beating along Main. He crossed back over to Front Street. That lone steamboat was loading by the light of flares and lanterns. It must be leaving within the week. Will was hunting now. He had to have sanctuary, and there was only one place in Fort Benton where he might hope to find it. Moreover, he wanted to fit one more piece into a puzzle, and thus he made his search. He called on the memory of that drunken night he and Buck Harper had spent in this town. He wove back and forth between Front and Main, only to decide each time that he had chosen the wrong side street. All this while he was alert for Littlejohn and certain that he heard a horse's movements not far away.

He grew desperate in his search and almost

gave it up. He thought of the livery stable and the little old man who'd been kind to him. He'd asked of that man a map and a curry-comb and a night's lodging, but he couldn't ask to be hidden from the law. And then he found himself before a clapboard building and knew it to be the one.

He let himself into the dim hallway and climbed the steep stairs as quietly as he could. He got into the narrow upper hall and groped along to the last door on the left. He wondered what time it was; he wondered if it were too late. He knocked, and Zoe opened the door and stood there with her wrapper clutched loosely about her and her perfume striking him.

"Ah, Will," she said with deep satisfaction. "I told you you'd come back."

He stepped into the room and pushed the door shut and put his back to it. He looked at Zoe; her sensuous face was shadowed by tiredness. He said, "Zoe, I'm on the dodge." He reached out and put his hands on her shoulders. "Am I safe here, Zoe?"

Boots beat against the stairs and fumbled along the hallway, stiffening Will with alarm. He crossed this tiny cubicle of a room in quick strides and extinguished the dim lamp burning on a stand near the bed. He whispered hoarsely, "You're not here, understand!"

How could he be sure of her loyalty? He stood in the heavy darkness and heard the drum of knuckles against the door. A man muttered drunkenly; he wondered if the man would try the door, and he cocked his fist and was ready. The man shuffled away. All this while Zoe had merely stood, a still presence.

When the boots had beat out their retreat, Will drew a deep breath. "A federal marshal named Littlejohn is combing the town for me," he said. "I've got to lie low till I can get away."

She gasped, and he judged then that she knew Littlejohn's name and reputation. He remembered the question he had come here to ask. "Zoe, why did Brant Millard mail money to Carrico?"

She said, "I know nothing about that, Will."

Every nerve in him was drawn taut. He needed her mercy and her protection, but he was beyond patience. He moved toward her and got hold of her wrist and squeezed hard. "Don't lie!" he snapped. "He came from the post office this afternoon and climbed into a carriage with you and spoke of the money. What does it mean, Zoe?"

She said, "You're hurting me, Will."

He let go of her wrist. "Zoe, I've got to know!"

She was silent for a moment. Then she said,

"A man hears many things at a card table, Will. And Carrico had a special interest in Matt Comfort — a special hatred for him — so Carrico asked questions when we first came to Fort Benton. He was told how Comfort had died aboard a steamboat, stabbed, supposedly by you, Will. He found out Comfort had been carrying a wooden Indian that had disappeared from the boat that same night. Carrico remembered that in St. Louis a man had sat in at one of the poker games when Comfort was there. Comfort had mentioned wanting a wooden Indian for his little girl and the man had told him where he might find one."

"Yes — ?" Will said.

"Carrico runs a game over on Front Street. One night that man played at his table."

"Brant Millard," Will said.

"Yes, Will. Carrico recognized him finally. He remembered that this man had put Comfort on the trail of a wooden Indian that had proved so valuable that Comfort was murdered for it. Carrico cornered Millard later and ran a bluff. A poker player knows how to bluff, Will. He reminded Millard of his talk in St. Louis with Comfort. He hinted that he, Carrico, knew a lot more about that wooden Indian than he was letting on. He said he'd be willing to forget the whole business for five thousand dollars."

"When was this?"

"About a year ago."

"Millard has been paying him ever since?"

"A hundred dollars a month. Millard argued that he didn't have five thousand dollars he could part with all in a chunk. Carrico settled for the hundred a month."

"He might as well have measured himself for a coffin, I think."

"Perhaps, Will. Carrico realized, of course, that a man in Millard's position could have raised the money. Millard has been stalling for time. Carrico has been very careful to keep off the range ever since and to make sure he has his back to a wall when he plays cards. And Millard has kept paying."

Will said, "I had to know. Littlejohn is after me for that murder eight years ago. I didn't do it, Zoe. But now I think I know who did. I've got to prove it. And I've got to stay here till it's safe to get out."

He crossed to the window and raised the shade and peered down. As much of the street as he could see was deserted. He thought of the relentless Littlejohn and debated as to whether he should try to get a livery stable horse and cut from town. But likely the livery stable would be locked for the night, the old man fast asleep. He thought of the hitchrails along the streets and wondered if he should risk stealing a horse. Damn' touchy business, that!

Zoe said, "I'll have to leave soon, Will. This is about the time I finish here, and Carrico will be expecting me. If he sees the light gone out and I don't come, he'll be up here to find out why. We have a little house on the edge of town. I'll steal away long enough tomorrow to bring you food."

He felt weary. He felt the shock of all the miles and the hours and the excitement. He wondered if he had enough edge left to try making a break tonight. He remembered the ten deputies the man in the restaurant had mentioned the day of the silver spike celebration. Littlejohn would have local law alerted by now; Littlejohn would have those deputies out combing the streets. Patience! Will had called on patience before, and he knew he had to call upon it again. He'd gain nothing if he ended up in the Fort Benton calaboose.

"I'll stay here," he said.

Zoe moved away from him in the darkness. She fumbled with her wrapper and was then a dim white blur; he heard the rustle of silk and knew she was dressing for the street. She came to him when she had finished and put her arms around him, and her lips found his. She kissed him; he kissed her in return. He

229

said, "There was no one else I could turn to, Zoe."

She said, "Will! Will!" Her lips were warm, but he caught no fire from them. He felt tender toward her; he felt grateful.

She moved away from him. "I'll have to lock the door behind me. I'll be back tomorrow."

She slipped out, and he heard the key grate. He moved to the window. The carriage was below now; he saw her walk along the street and climb into the carriage. This old building creaked. He sat down on the edge of the bed. He wondered if Trixie and the other girls had left. He stretched out upon the bed and was alert to every sound. He wondered if he'd made a mistake in not trying to get out of town tonight.

This, then, was what it was like to be a fugitive, this being jumpy and uncertain and afraid of shadows. It harked his mind back to those first days after he'd quitted the *Cherokee;* it brought him memories from all the wary years. But never had Sam Littlejohn been so close on his heels as now. He turned over in his mind all the things Littlejohn had told him on the trail. He placed these together and added to them what he had learned from Zoe. He thought about Littlejohn as he had come to know the man on the trail from Diamond C, a curious mixture of zeal and sentimentality, forthrightness and suspicion, stubbornness and flexibility. And then he slept. . . .

Sunlight stood at the single window when he awoke. He lay for a moment, surprised at his whereabouts. There'd been a steamboat mixed into his dreaming. He ran a hand over his cheeks and chin and felt the rasp of stubble. He was hungry and thirsty. He began to pace the room, feeling closed in. He wanted to batter at the walls. He hated this room; the smell of bedbugs and sin was here.

He risked peering from behind the window curtains and saw men moving along the street, and an occasional woman. A dog lay out in the road sunning himself; a little boy rolled a hoop. Will tried to get a glimpse of the sun; it appeared to be directly overhead. He began pacing again, then willed himself to lie on the bed. Its springs complained at his weight. He dozed a little, but all the while he was listening for Zoe's footsteps on the stairs. At last they came.

The key rattled and she let herself in. She was wearing a skirt and jacket that matched, and a hat fancy as any he'd seen on the grand ladies of Pine Street in St. Louis. But by daylight she looked older than she should. She'd brought him cold meat and bread and a pint whiskey flask which now held water. She sat watching while he ate.

He had asked her one question last night; there was still the other, older one. But first he said, "You must know Carrico very well now."

She spread her hands. "What was I to do, Will?"

He said, "I didn't mean it to sound like an accusation. It's only that I wondered how much he might have got around to telling you. Did he ever speak about me — about the orphanage where he got me?"

"No, Will."

"Not one word that might have given some idea who my people were?"

She looked at him curiously. "That's still very important to you, isn't it?"

"So important that when I come face to face with Carrico, I'm going to ask him."

They were both silent then. She appeared nervous, fumbling with the gloves she carried. "Your horse is impounded at the livery stable," she said. "The talk is that the horse must have stumbled and dumped you out of the saddle. A deputy found the bay grazing near the fort. Littlejohn said it was yours." She let her words trail away; then she added very casually, "Littlejohn has posted a thousand dollars reward for you."

"Dead or alive?"

"He wants you alive."

He frowned. "I've got to get out of here for your sake as well as mine. I don't want you in trouble. Could you do a couple more things for me? Rent a saddle horse and leave it somewhere close by when night comes. That will be better than my raising a hullabaloo by stealing a horse. If anything goes wrong, you can say you rented a horse with the idea of taking a night off and going riding. I stole the horse. In fact, after I've had an hour's start, you'd better report the horse missing. And bring me a gun, too."

She said, "Yes, Will."

Shortly she left, not kissing him this time. He felt lonely once the door was again locked. He waited through an endless afternoon. He thought of the question he had asked Zoe about the orphanage, and his hands opened and closed. Carrico was the one person with the answer. He, Will, would have that answer some day, for he would force it from Carrico, if need be. He thought of many things — the reward Littlejohn had posted, and the fact that the bay hadn't been hurt. He was glad about the horse.

After the dragging hours, darkness came. He watched it grow at the window, and he saw lights spring up along the street. People down there, going about their quiet business.

People heading home for supper or walking toward a night's pleasure. People who didn't have to glance over their shoulders or start at every sound. He wondered what it would be like to walk so carelessly, to know the simple comfort of freedom.

He waited in growing impatience for the footsteps upon the stairs. Finally he heard them. He moved toward the door, but the key that rattled was in another lock down the hall. Trixie? Again he waited, and again footsteps came. He was sure they were Zoe's, and then he wasn't sure. The footsteps beat along the hallway and the key scratched, and Zoe slipped in.

She was wearing a cloak this evening. From under it she produced a Colt's forty-five. She said in a strained voice, "Here's your gun." She didn't hand it to him; she stepped close and dropped it into his holster. "I loaded it for you," she said.

"The horse?" he asked.

"At a hitchrail on Front Street. A roan gelding. Just around the corner."

"Do you know whether Littlejohn is in town?"

"Talk is that he rode out. But a lot of people are after that reward."

Guilt stood on her face. He saw it now. He lifted the gun from his holster and broke the gun open. It was empty. "A lot of people," he said. His voice was low and terrible. "And you're one of them."

She stepped back from him, her eyes growing frightened and one hand rising to her cheek. Anger welled in him, and he wanted to strike her. He half raised his hand and then let it fall, for suddenly he pitied her more than he had ever pitied any other human being. Whatever his nameless heritage, he was better off than she was. He said, with a shake of his head, "If I ever wonder what I was worth to you, I'll know. One thousand dollars." He plucked shells from his cartridge belt and loaded the gun. "Don't raise a scream, or I'll come back and kill you. Good-by, Zoe."

He went down the hallway fast, and he took the stairs fast. When he came out upon the darkened street, he saw the carriage waiting just where it had been that night he and Buck had walked away from here. He knew that Carrico would be in that carriage, and he knew how Will Yeoman would be expected to act. He'd told Zoe he'd put a question to Carrico when they met, but he hadn't added that he intended to be a free man first. They had schemed that now he wouldn't be able to resist what looked like opportunity, and that he'd walk up to the carriage and throw a gun on Carrico and ask him the question. But it would be an empty gun, and Carrico would show him his derringer. A thousand dollars worth of derringer.

He did walk directly to the carriage, and he did lean into it, gun in hand, but he said, "The gun's loaded, Carrico. Make no mistake. Zoe's face gave her away."

Carrico's expression turned slack with surprise. Carrico knew him full well: after the eight years Carrico knew him, because Carrico had been expecting him, and in the man's recognition lay the last proof that Zoe had betrayed him. There'd be no roan gelding waiting on Front Street.

Will wrapped his free hand in Carrico's fancy shirt front. Carrico cursed and tried to shake the derringer out of his sleeve. Will batted at the tiny gun and sent it clattering to the floorboards of the carriage. Carrico raised a yell. Will hauled him up from the seat and jerked him out into the street. He sent Carrico sprawling with a shove of his hand.

Then Will was clambering up into the carriage. He unwrapped the reins from around the whipstock and plucked the whip from its socket and lashed at the team. Carrico's yell was in his ears as he wheeled around the corner and clattered up Front Street. Someone caught up the yell and echoed it, and Will saw men running out to converge upon him. But he'd raised the team to a gallop, and people fell back before his furious coming. He swept past them and was soon beyond the fort and hitting the river trail that led northward.

16

The Thundering Dust

That last steamboat had left the Benton levee. Sweeping along Front Street, Will had seen from the corner of his eye that the packet was gone, and for a moment he'd been amazed. From Zoe's room, he'd heard no departing whistle nor sensed any of the excitement that usually attended a leave-taking, but now he realized that the packet must have pulled out while he'd been asleep that morning. He remembered how a steamboat had been in his dreaming. He laid the whip across the backs of Carrico's team.

This trail was no wagon road, and the carriage lurched and swayed over the roughness. Pursuit would be coming, Will knew, drawn by the reward Littlejohn had posted as well as by the excitement of the chase. He fled through the night. A good pair of horses up ahead, but he was demanding everything of them; he was spending them recklessly. When he glanced back, he could see nothing in the darkness, but this did not lessen his alarm. How much time had he gained?

The carriage struck a rock, one wheel bouncing high. Will, flung the width of the seat, fought for balance. The vehicle careened on. Will peered for other hazards ahead. He'd lost track of time and distance. How far, he wondered. He looked for landmarks. His mind raced ahead to that steamboat somewhere downriver, the steamboat Brant Millard had planned to board. Small chance of overtaking the packet by following this river trail.

What he needed, Will knew, was a saddle horse. Then he could cut overland and so gain an edge on the boat, which had to follow the windings of the Missouri. No moon yet tonight, and the sky was cloudy again. That meant the boat would be likely to tie up to the bank. Somewhere downriver it was probably choking a stump right now. He still had a chance.

Then a wheel struck a sharp rock, and even above the clatter of hoofs and the creak of the carriage he heard the splintering of wood.

He hauled on the reins and brought the team to a standstill. Leaping out, he scraped a

239

match aglow and saw the splintered spokes. He shook his head, dismayed; disappointment ran through him. He stood in the night and listened, sure that he heard the drumming of hoofs along the backtrail, faint and far away. He knelt and put an ear to the ground. Riders coming.

Easy, now! he told himself. Easy, or panic would have its hold on him.

He moved up to the team and looked at the spent, lathered horses. He had never used any animal so before, and he laid his hand on one of the horses soothingly. He wondered if either horse had been broken to ride; he wondered if he could cut one loose and fashion a hackamore out of harness leather. But there was no more running left in the horses, and Will knew it. And he was losing precious time. He looked about him at the river and the lift of the land and was sure the contours of bluff and bend were familiar to him. He judged he was very near the fork of the trail where he'd parted from Libbie.

He made his choice then. He struck out overland toward B-M Connected. He left the trail and picked his way across the uneven ground, hurrying, but often pausing to listen.

He guessed how it would be with the pursuers. Soon they would come clattering up to mill around the buggy. They would spend many matches searching the ground for sign. They would debate, some wanting to go this way and some that, and then they would begin hunting. Likely they would argue that he would keep to the back country and concealment.

He trudged on, walking swiftly, almost running. He'd covered this cut-off from the river trail just yesterday and found it not too long, but afoot it seemed endless. He caught his heel in a gopher hole; he began limping. The moon finally showed, the light making his going a little easier; but he was glad the sky was still cloudy. He didn't want to be skylined. He felt winded; his chest hurt and his boots pinched. But he kept going until the land dropped away before him, and he found himself upon that low ridge where he'd looked down on B-M's buildings yesterday and seen Buck Harper ride away.

No light showed in bunkhouse or ranch house; only the cook-shack windows stood yellow against the night. No sound rose from down there; it was a ghost ranch.

He broke into a run again. He came sprinting down the slant, heading straight for the house. He mounted the gallery and let himself into the hallway. He thrust open the door to the living room and called Millard's name. Darkness lay here, and silence. He left the

241

house and hurried across to the wagon shed.

The light spring wagon into which he and Blucher had loaded a box was gone.

He ran to the corrals; all were empty save the breaking corral where El Capitan fretted. He looked into the barn and found it empty, too.

What had happened struck him like the blow of a fist. Millard had left, taking the wagon and its cargo overland to the river. And the crew was gone, too, every last man of them, and that meant that Blucher had chosen tonight to strike at Diamond C.

The cook opened the door of his shack and stood against the light, peering across the yard. Will called to him, then moved toward the man. Will asked, "Did the crew head for the river?"

The cook said guardedly, "All but a couple that's holding the beef gather." He didn't look at Will in the manner of a disinterested person greeting a hand just returned from a Fort Benton spree. He was too wary, this cook, and Will realized that the impression he'd taken pains to leave with the bunkhouse bunch had misfired. Had word come from Fort Benton during the day that Will Yeoman was a wanted man? He said sharply, "So they've gone to Diamond C."

The cook's old face turned wooden. "I've

242

wrangled grub for a lot of ranches in my day. My job is only to see they get fed. I don't concern myself with the skallyhootin'."

Will said, "But Millard left to catch the packet."

The cook shrugged. "That wouldn't be any secret. A steamboat roustabout rode out about dawn to carry word from the captain that they'd be taking off."

Will said, "Look, I need a horse as bad as any man ever needed one. There's only one horse here. Will you help me get a saddle onto El Capitan?"

The cook's face livened. Then he frowned. He was making his own debate, Will judged, as to whether the request held for him any violation of his self-imposed neutrality. But something like admiration moved in the cook's eyes; something turned the cook young. "If you're crazy enough to try that horse, I'm just crazy enough to help you." He jerked off his floursack apron and tossed it aside with a flourish.

"Come on," Will said.

He strode toward the corral. Here was another of those calls on courage where the trick was not to think of consequences. Pause once, and he was done for. He knew this with a terrible certainty. He got to the corral and found a rope looped over a gate post. The cook, who'd headed for the barn, now loomed up carrying another rope and a hackamore. He held a saddle perched on one hip. El Capitan was on the far side of the corral. Will opened the gate and slipped inside, the cook after him.

"It's been a hell of a long time," the cook said, "since I did any cowboying."

El Capitan had come alert. He stood with head upraised and nostrils flaring, wild and beautiful and deadly in the half-light. Will shook out the noose and sent it singing. The noose settled over the stallion's head, and the horse charged him. Will moved swiftly, following the wall of the corral and trying to keep slack out of the rope. He didn't hear the swish of the cook's rope, but the old man's frightened cry came to him as El Capitan whirled about and headed across the corral, thundering toward the cook. The rope in Will's hand tautened. He dug in the spike heels of his boots and held. The cook had got a second loop over the stallion's head, and they fought the horse between them.

They got the stallion snubbed to the post, but hobbling him and slipping the saddle on and off till the horse stood shuddering, no longer fighting the saddle, took time. Will stood panting, his shirt clinging to him with sweat. How much of the night was gone? He looked for the Dog Star and made his guess, and then he called to the cook, "Get safe away." He eased up into the saddle and the cook removed the rope.

The surprising thing was that for a moment El Capitan only stood. In that moment Will found time to wonder at his own folly. Then something hit the horse as a spark hits powder. He began plunging in a series of crowhops about the corral, heedless of harm to himself. Will had seen a blind bucker go over a bluff with its rider, not caring about anything but shedding the man in the saddle. He was riding such a horse now.

He called on all the skill he had. He'd done very little horse breaking at the ranches where he'd worked, but he'd found the toughest horses to be those that some other rider had started to break. El Capitan was such a one. El Capitan was bucking hard and high. There was nothing to do but hang on and hope and rely on instinct.

El Capitan tried to scrape him off against the fence. He got a leg out of stirrup just in time. The horse swapped ends and rose high, sunfishing as he came down. Will felt the jar in his teeth. The driving thud-thud-thud of hoofs, stirring thunder in the dust, made a steady beat in Will's brain. He thought he heard the cook yell encouragement; he didn't even know where the cook had perched himself.

The man who would ride this horse would be more desperate than the horse, Brant Millard had once said. That desperation was Will's.

The sky was a wheeling, crazy thing; the dust rose and choked him. The dust was a silver mist. He tried to get his neckerchief up over his nose but failed. He was being battered as though by a hammer; he was getting to the limit of what he could endure. He met each movement of the horse with the dismal knowledge that his own movements were growing sluggish, his reactions entirely too slow. But still he stuck. He stuck until at last El Capitan stood on trembling legs, heaving and blowing, his head down and the fight gone out of him.

"You rode him," the cook shouted from a top rail. His arms flapped like a scarecrow's. "By God, you rode him!"

Will slipped down from the saddle. He tied the stallion to a rail of the corral and walked outside. He sat down heavily on the ground and put his head between his knees, too weary for whatever must come next. He knew he should be up and going. He sat for a long time.

After a while the cook came and stood by

him. The cook said, "Riders coming," and moved toward his cook-shack, fading into obscurity, fading into neutrality.

Will stood up feeling like a man dragged from a deep and sluggish sleep. He shook his head. That posse from Fort Benton? But no, he judged from the beat of hoofs that only two or three riders were coming in. Diamond C men? He felt for the gun Zoe had given him; the gun was gone. He'd lost it in that ride he'd made. He peered into the breaking corral, hoping to catch the glint of moonlight on metal, but the gun could be anywhere, trampled in the dust.

He ran toward the bunkhouse. Stepping into the dark interior, he lighted a match and began rummaging about in search of a spare gun some B-M hand might have left. There was a Winchester on an elkhorn rack over the door, but he wanted a hand gun. He found a forty-five in a tangle of blankets on one of the bunks. He checked the loads and turned about as the riders came clattering into the yard.

Two of them.

He wondered if they would notice that El Capitan was saddled and tied. But no, as saddle leather squealed, one of the riders dropped down, and boots came beating across the yard straight to the bunkhouse. A man in a mighty big hurry, from the sound. The fellow came in and groped his way to the lamp and lighted it. As he replaced the chimney and turned up the wick, his shadow sprang huge along the wall. The lamp's glow highlighted his forehead, and the stubbled, truculent jaw stood plainly outlined.

From a corner of the room, Will said, "Hello, Henry."

Blucher wheeled about, his face awry with astonishment. He was a scared man and an angry one, hate-ridden. He dropped his hand toward his holster, but Will waggled the gun he held and stepped close to Blucher and said, "Don't do it, Henry."

Blucher's shoulders slumped; he was, Will judged, harried by more than what this moment held. He had come in hard-breathing, like one pursued; he had made a fumbling business out of lighting the lamp. He said, staring at Will, "Damn it, who are you anyway?"

Will said, "So you made your strike at Diamond C." He spoke softly; he was mindful of that other man out in the yard. Noonan? Moffat or Beal or the Yellowstone Kid? "You're home early and empty-handed, Henry."

Blucher cursed. "Damn you! It blew up in our faces. She'd got Clark's help, and Littlejohn's. We'd hoped to hit before that happened. Noonan woke up and heard you talking to the girl by the haystack. We hadn't figured on Littlejohn. The boys went to pieces when they found him against them."

So Noonan had heard. That explained why the cook had been wary tonight. But Will felt a warm elation that Littlejohn had chosen to go back to Diamond C. All that talking on the trail to Benton hadn't been wasted. He forgave Littlejohn for everything across the years. He smiled grimly at Blucher. "And you're here to roll your soogans," Will guessed. "You're riding off this range before Littlejohn collars you. So that's it!"

Blucher asked again, "Damn' you, who the hell are you?"

"Will Yeoman."

Blucher's mouth loosened with surprise, and his eyes showed how guilty his knowledge was.

"The name hits you," Will said. "I'd guess that you were in that yawl eight years ago when Millard lowered the wooden Indian from the *Cherokee*. Millard didn't dare take passage on the packet, not with Littlejohn aboard. Millard must have come upriver, either by horse or by a faster packet and caught up with the *Cherokee* in Dakota. Matt Comfort had to die, of course. He probably recognized Millard in the fight in the cabin."

Blucher said nothing. His eyes held fast on Will; his tongue came out and ran along his lips.

"One thing fooled me all along," Will said. "This place only went through the motions of being a ranch, but I didn't guess it was the river's end rendezvous of the wrecking gang. Not till I remembered the box. Now I see why you wanted to drive the Comforts from their river acreage. You wanted a location where the last steamers could be looted almost at your front door."

Outside, that second rider was dismounting. Will heard the creak of gear. Had the fellow heard the voices, or was he merely wondering what was keeping Blucher?

"Millard's gone downriver," Will said softly. "To the last meeting of the gang. I'm going after him, Blucher. I'm going to get him for what he did to Matt Comfort. And because he's got that wooden Indian with him."

Blucher said nothing. Instead, Blucher tried for his gun.

Will raised his own gun and brought the barrel down hard across Blucher's skull. He put force into the blow. Blucher's knees buckled, and Will moved closer and caught him and eased him down gently, mindful of that man outside. Littlejohn could wrap up Blucher for delivery. But still there was Millard. And still there was that other rider out in the yard.

He stepped cautiously toward the bunkhouse door. He stood listening, and he heard the scrape of a boot sole against the ground.

Buck Harper said, "You might as well come on out, Will. But get this straight: I'm one of the B-M boys now. Just be sure you come empty-handed."

17

Downriver

He supposed he should be shocked that Buck was here and siding B-M, but he wasn't. Not after the first blow of recognition. It was a natural thing — natural as Sam Littlejohn's turning up in Diamond C's yard after the years to put a gun at Will's back. All men ran true to their breed, and Buck's way was the easy way and the one that promised the most to Buck. This Will had known always and never before faced, remembering only Buck's smile and his warm way. Libbie had said that he didn't really like Buck, but even then he hadn't been sure. Now he knew, and a coldness gathered in him.

He said, "I saw you here the other day. I might have guessed."

Buck said, "Oh, that. I rode over on Diamond C business. Millard sized me up and liked my cut. He said he could use a man in Diamond C's bunkhouse. He talked pronto money, not the kind the Comforts may get around to paying some day. He even laid some of it on the line. I savvy money, Will."

"And when the raid came off tonight, you put your gun with B-M's."

"My idea was to hold back and see who came out ahead. The winning side would have been my side. But when Sam Littlejohn rode out to Diamond C today, I knew it was time to cut loose. They haven't got my face on any dodger, Will, but I had to leave a couple towns fast, and my description may have got around. Littlejohn would remember where most men wouldn't."

Will said, "I told you you were no damn' good, Buck."

Buck said soothingly, "Hell, Will, there's no need for trouble between us. There's a lot I don't understand, but I just heard you tell Blucher you were going after Millard. Something about a wooden Indian. You had a wooden Indian on the brain once before. I'm not asking questions, kid. But I reckon Millard would pay me to keep you off his back. All you have to do is be reasonable. Come on out, Will."

Will came out. He came through the doorway with the gun in his hand.

The suddenness of his coming gave him a slight edge. He knew at once that Buck hadn't expected fight from him. Buck stood there in the yard with his sharp face surprised, looking as if he didn't quite believe what he saw. Then he changed and became the dangerous man Will had glimpsed for a moment that day before the store they'd meant to rob. Buck tried for his gun and got it out of leather.

He was fast, Buck. He brought up the gun and fired all in one swift motion, but Will fired first, taking a quick sidestep. Buck's bullet thunked into the bunkhouse wall near Will's shoulder. He saw Buck double over and drop his gun and take a couple of crazy steps forward and then go down in a heap.

Buck pulled himself to his hands and knees and looked up at Will and shook his head. "I didn't think you'd do it," Buck said distinctly. "I surely didn't, kid." He said this and sprawled forward and died.

Will stared, and felt as though he were going to be sick. He'd never thought he'd kill a man, and this man was Buck who'd ridden all those miles with him; this was Buck who'd been his partner. Or had he been? Cat and dog, the old hostler in Fort Benton had said, Will remembered. Maybe from the first he and Buck had ridden different trails, even when they were stirrup to stirrup. Once before he'd thought he might have to fight Buck. Now he realized that his kind of man had been born to fight Buck's kind.

But that didn't make Buck any the less dead here in the yard.

The crash of guns had brought the cook-shack door cautiously open. Will turned Buck over and straightened him out. Then he lifted Buck and carried him into the bunkhouse and put him in a bunk. Blucher still lay heaped upon the floor. Will went to the corral and got one of the ropes that had been laid on El Capitan and came back and tied up Blucher. Will was sure Littlejohn would be coming. Then he walked out into the yard. The cook stood there peering.

"One dead," Will said.

The cook shook his head. "When dead men start getting strewed around, I head for a new job." He looked at Blucher's horse and Buck's, standing ground-anchored in the yard. "I'll put one of these horses up and take the other. I'll leave it at one of the Benton livery stables, if anybody should ask."

"Good luck to you," Will said. "I'm riding, too."

There was still Brant Millard. Odd that he still couldn't remember Millard from Carrico's place. Too many faces.

He, Will, hadn't been excited when he'd overheard Millard tell Blucher of his intention of going downriver. A score of reasons might

255

have been taking a Montana rancher on such a trip. But since then he'd heard Littlejohn talk of the river-wreckers, and he'd remembered the box, and he'd forced from Zoe the fact that Millard had been the man who'd put Matt Comfort on the trail of a wooden Indian. That Indian was now going downriver. Millard was returning it to St. Louis for that last split-up before the organization dissolved; he was keeping the Indian handy lest another need arise to smuggle loot past lawmen.

And Will Yeoman knew what he must do. He couldn't chance that Millard would be bagged in St. Louis. Millard had slipped out of one such trap years ago. Besides, there was a personal debt to be collected. He had Matt Comfort's death to remember, but more, too. There were Libbie and Mrs. Comfort who had suffered from Millard's scheming, and there was the law of Marshal Sam Littlejohn that had hunted Millard so long. Thus had all the threads drawn together into a single strand.

He might have taken Blucher's horse or Buck's, but both had covered many miles tonight. He got a bridle from the barn and forced it onto El Capitan, speaking soothingly to the horse; he swung up into the saddle. The stallion flinched and made a few awkward bucks. Will lifted his hand to the cook and then lined out in a general northeasterly direction, heading toward the Missouri.

He had made no mistake in his choice of mounts. He had a horse with staying power beneath him. He thundered across the miles, and light began to show in the east, spreading slowly, driving away the night. He rode into the dawn. He had no idea how far the steamboat might have got; it would make good time going downstream, but he could only guess at what hour it had left Benton and how many stops it had made since. He called on patience again. First he would reach the river and then begin his search.

The early light was gray, dimmed by river mist. He rode along through wreaths of fog. Somewhere that Fort Benton posse smelled along a trail and somewhere Sam Littlejohn rode, probably with Diamond C's crew and Clark's crew behind him, but Will saw no one. He wished he could close his mind to Buck lying dead, but Buck stayed with him. The memory of Buck, bullet shattered and making his last say, was strong in his mind; he wondered if this would always be so.

He came upon a rough road; and since it led in the direction of the Missouri, he followed along it. The sun showed itself in the east, hazy and red; the sun climbed higher and began to dispel the fog, and out of the shredding mist Will rode to find himself atop the bluffs with the river below.

He looked down upon that brown, snaky stream but could see little because of the fog streamers that still lay thick along the water. Most likely the boat was downstream from here. He harked up a memory of the map the Fort Benton hostler had drawn for him, and he recalled that the river made a wide bend to the north before it reached the mouth of Big Sandy Creek and Citadel Rock. He frowned, faced with a choice. If he forded the river, he could cut overland, still striking to the northeast and so reach a place where he must surely be ahead of the boat. The land miles would be fewer than the river miles. Better such a maneuver than following the river the long way on this side. But first he had to find a place where he could get down to the bank, and then he had to find fording.

He began walking the horse along the crest of the bluffs, moving downriver. Close to the water the fog fanned and broke and settled weirdly. He thought he heard a faint, muffled sound, and he brought El Capitan to a stand, listening. A commotion somewhere, for sure, but there was no placing the sound. He rode on.

After a mile he came to where the land dropped away, giving him access to the river. Yonder another road looped down to a small wooden pier and a shack of sorts, and he thought of the Diamond C landing Millard had mentioned, but he knew he must be too far north for that. Clark's place? He peered out across the face of the waters. The fog was lifting, and a vast bulk emerged out of the fog and took shape. He saw the twin funnels of a packet, a mountain boat like the *Cherokee*, and he saw the twin spars that jutted up on either side of the boat. He knew what sound he'd heard; the commotion came more clearly to him now and was a remembered thing out of the years. Yonder boat had beached itself upon a sandbar and was grasshoppering off.

Here was luck, and he accepted it gratefully. He could guess what had happened. The captain, making a start so late in the season, had probably been fearful of being frozen in and so had risked a night run under a cloudy sky. And he'd got his boat stranded for his trouble. No matter; the packet was here, and with that realization something soared in him, heady and heartening.

No river in the world would have been wide enough to stop him now. He touched spur to El Capitan and sent loose rock rolling as he came galloping down the slant, scorning the long loops of the road. He got to the river bank and hit the wooden landing at full tilt, thundering out upon the planking. He gave the stallion the spur again, forcing the mount off the pier and into the river. The shock of the water was cold, bitterly cold.

El Capitan struggled out toward the steamboat. Will gritted his teeth against the cold. The current tugged at him and pulled him from the saddle. He grasped at the saddlehorn and let the stallion tow him. Lying low in the water as he was, the steamboat now seemed far away to Will. But the current was with horse and man, sweeping them toward the sandbar, sweeping them onto the bar.

Will struggled to a muddy footing, his boots going deep. Above him the boat loomed, deck upon deck, and he heard the close thunder as the paddlewheel churned so futilely. He saw faces lined along the rails, and he put a hand out to the main deck, which sat not very high, for these flat-built packets drew only three or four feet of water.

Hands were stretched to help him. Passengers who had witnessed horse and man swimming had crowded to the lower deck. People jabbered at him, but he couldn't hear them above the thunder of the paddles. A big red-faced man leaped to the bar and snatched at El Capitan's trailing reins. Someone pounded Will's back. He guessed that these people figured he was some cowhand who wanted downriver passage and had missed the boat at

Benton. His teeth were chattering, but he was no longer conscious of being cold. He shook off the friendly hands and shouldered hastily through the crowd and started up a companionway to the boiler deck.

He had never been aboard this boat before, but he knew it as a man knows the face of an old friend. This packet was sister to the *Cherokee* he'd explored with a boy's eagerness. And he knew where he'd likely find Millard. The first-class cabins were on the boiler deck. Millard would have bought the best.

Halfway up the steps, he felt the thrust of excitement. Millard was above. And the wooden case Millard had brought aboard stood upended near the companionway at the boiler deck's rail. Evidently Millard hadn't yet made room for the case in his cabin but wasn't trusting it with the general cargo on the main deck.

Millard looked down at him and was no longer sleepy eyed. Millard's face showed taut and angry, and Will saw him now as a ruthless man, cruel enough to have threatened to send his foreman into El Capitan's corral, cruel enough to have made war against two women, cruel enough to have done murder once. Millard was also an alarmed man. Will wondered if something in his own face was giving Millard warning, or if Millard was remembering

Noonan's report. There were no words between them, yet Millard was bringing a gun from beneath his coat.

Will's rode at his hip, but he didn't know whether it was water-fouled. He didn't try for the gun. He came up the steps relentlessly, and Millard fired at him. Will felt the burn of the bullet along his ribs. The impact tore at him, but he'd got a hard hold on the handrail. With his free hand he jerked out his own gun and hurled it at Millard's gun arm, knocking the weapon from Millard's hand.

Millard turned as though to run, and Will cried, "Wait, damn you!"

Millard began tugging at the wooden case leaning against the rail. He hauled the case to the companionway and gave it a shove, toppling it downward. Will saw it coming; it loomed big, blocking out the sight of Millard. Will veered to one side, the case striking his shoulder a blow and hurtling by him to crash on the lower deck. Will took one look and saw the case splintered open. Eight years now since he'd last glimpsed that wooden Indian.

He leaped on up the companionway. He was a man with no thought for consequences; he had waited too long for this moment to weigh anything into it but the need to get his hands on Millard. This, too, must have stood out on him, for panic showed on Millard's face now. He stooped to pick up his gun. Will came at him just as Millard got the gun and brought it up. Flame burst at Will. Shock ran through his hip. He closed with Millard and wrenched the gun from the man and hurled it overboard. Locked together, the two of them careened against the rail.

Millard shouted, raising a cry for help. Millard's face was contorted. Will laughed at him.

Holding tight to Millard, Will found all of this struggle familiar. It was the same old fight repeated, the two of them battling against the rail of a boiler deck, the one trying to haul the other to the planking. But there was a difference, too, made from all the years between. Will sensed that difference and gloried in it. He wasn't Will Yeoman, St. Louis stripling, battling a man of superior strength. He was Will Yeoman who'd seen the shining mountains and put his shoulder to the bogged wheels along the Bozeman Trail and done a prospector's shovel work and stood over a blacksmith's anvil. He was a man who'd worn a cowboy's garb and battled through the hard winter and won strength from the fight. He was a man hardened by adversity and sharpened by a fugitive's constant wariness — a man trained, unwittingly, across all the rawhide years for this second chance at Brant Millard.

Two bullets had found him, and he knew they must be draining his strength, but he didn't feel the loss. Not yet. The old fury rode him, the fury that had sent him after Millard that night when Matt Comfort had lain in his own blood aboard the *Cherokee*. Between clenched teeth, he said, "Do you know me, Millard? Do you know me?" Millard made no answer, but his eyes told Will he remembered.

Will got his hands on Millard's throat. Heedless of Millard's flailing arms, he squeezed hard, bending Millard backward across the rail. He saw Millard's face turn red; he saw the man's tongue protruding, but still he increased the pressure of his fingers. He wondered if Millard felt helpless, utterly alone, remembering Blucher and the others he could call upon who would not hear.

Will became aware that men had come stampeding to the boiler deck; they were swarming about him, trying to tear him from Millard. He saw the blue and brass of the captain's uniform and heard the captain's wild bellow. He let go of Millard then, and the man fell unconscious to the deck.

"Lock him up, Captain," Will said. "Sam Littlejohn wants him. And put the Indian in a safe place. Belongs to a little girl . . . "

He knew that last sounded crazy, but he

saw the captain nod. "Littlejohn's on the bank right now, sitting a saddle and waving his hat," the captain said. "I'll put a yawl overboard. We'll get the straight of this shortly."

Blucher had talked. Blucher must have told Littlejohn where Will Yeoman could be found. That must have been the way of it. But Will couldn't hold to coherent thinking; the weight of Millard's bullets seemed to be dragging him down. Hands were reaching to steady him, but the darkness crowded close and he went drifting downward into it. He knew that he was smiling as he fell . . .

18

True to Breed

Snow swirled against the windows of Diamond C's ranch house to cling soft and sticky to the glass, but in this bedroom he had occupied these last three weeks Will was warm and snug. He lay here restless. He'd got a little tired of being propped up against pillows and tended by Libbie and her mother as carefully as a sick calf. And he didn't like the idea that the Comforts were having to sleep in a lean-to while he occupied their bed. The notion crowded at some man-pride. In other days he had bedded often on the ground and found it good enough.

He could smell medicine on himself, but there was only a stiffness of muscles where Millard's bullets had torn him. He'd got to thinking lately that he'd like to get into his clothes. He meant to tell Libbie so when the chance came.

She'd come into the bedroom to read him a

letter fetched by fast horse from Yankton. It was a long letter from Sam Littlejohn, who'd reached that Dakota port by the very packet Millard had taken. Will lay watching Libbie as she read. She had a firm chin, he decided, but not a stubborn one, and her hair would be more red than brown with sunlight caught in it. She was nearing the end of the letter, the music of her voice soft and steady.

" . . . And so to sum up, Will, the case is now closed that occupied my time for over ten years. With the bagging of the B-M crew and the subsequent capture of Blucher and Millard, the Montana end of the ring was corraled. The latest downriver report indicates that Millard was a top man in the organization. And adds the good word that a very successful raid was staged at St. Louis. Much of the loot has been recovered and some restitution can be made. A great deal of the credit belongs to you, and I have indicated so in my official report. Had it not been for your pursuit of Millard, developments might have gone otherwise. I confess that I would not have attached so much importance to Millard. I'd have spent my time running down stragglers from B-M rather than heading back to the river, as I did when I got news from Blucher about you. Blucher, wanting you arrested, was eager enough to put me on your trail.

"That you did not choose to tell me on the outskirts of Fort Benton your full suspicion concerning Millard I can readily understand. I had not earned your trust. For whatever harm I did you by thought or word or action in the past, I hope you will forgive me. If you choose to continue thinking of me as a heartless, stubborn man, that is your right; but I hope you will remember that I chose friendship ahead of duty a second time and went to the aid of the Comforts. That such a step proved to have forwarded my pursuit of the river-wreckers was, of course, fortunate.

"If you are interested in wearing a law badge, I am sure I could help you officially toward such a goal. Do let me know. Please accept my heartiest regards and pass along my good wishes to Hagar and Elizabeth. Most sincerely. Samuel R. Littlejohn."

Libbie folded the letter carefully and returned it to the envelope. She smiled at Will. "You seem to have a job waiting, if you want it."

He had known that he was a free man ever since the day Littlejohn had boarded the packet to take Millard into custody; yet he'd been a fugitive so long that freedom still seemed strange, even with the confirmation of the letter. He smiled back at Libbie. He had come to know this girl very well in the weeks he'd been recuperating here after Littlejohn had had him sent overland from the packet. In fever he'd felt her hands soothingly upon him. He had listened each day for her footfalls and looked forward to the time she spent at his bedside. He had even invented little excuses to keep her in this room. And he had told her everything about himself.

He said now, "No law badge for me. I'd rather be a rancher."

"There will always be a place for you here, Will." She laid the envelope on the table beside his bed. She hesitated, and then, without looking squarely at him, she said, "Rube Freeman brought news from town. Just something he picked up on the street, where all the gossip belongs to everybody. That girl you told me about, that Zoe, is leaving."

This did not surprise him. Zoe would go where Carrico went, and for Carrico a paying game had played out with Brant Millard's capture. *Let them go,* he thought. But he had to see Carrico; he could not deny a need he'd lived with so long. He looked up at Libbie. "I feel able to be out of bed," he said. "I've got to go to town."

She said, "Of course, Will," but her eyes shadowed, and he supposed she was thinking he wanted to say good-by to Zoe in spite of everything. He did not tell her how it really was.

He had something he intended to ask of Libbie, but first he had to see Carrico and put the question to him and then he could do all his talking to Libbie.

When she'd left the room, closing the door quietly, he got into his clothes. They fitted him loosely, and he judged that he'd lost weight. He looked in the bedroom mirror and saw a face gaunted down. He felt strong enough, though, even if he was a bit tottery.

He came out into the parlor and spoke to Mrs. Comfort, who sat in her rocking chair. She liked him, he knew. He owed her for much kindness these past weeks. She smiled and said, "You look mighty spry for a sick man." He started for the door, and she said, "If you're going outside, you'll need a heavy coat."

"I had one, but I must have left it at B-M," he said.

"That old sheepskin hanging on the peg belonged to my husband," she said. "Help yourself to it."

"Thanks," he said and took the sheepskin down and shrugged into it. Thus did he don Matt Comfort's coat.

He went out into the yard. Freeman and Lum Garvey were not in sight; but old Pablo, muffled in an ancient buffalo coat, was pottering about.

El Capitan frisked in a corral; Will's bay stood stolidly in another. Littlejohn had had El Capitan sent here from the river, and the bay had been fetched from the Fort Benton livery stable by one of the Diamond C hands. Will guessed he owned El Capitan now, his by right of conquest. But he didn't feel up to riding El Capitan today. To Pablo he said, "Will you saddle up the bay for me?"

"*Si*," Pablo said and went about the task.

Will stood in the yard waiting, a leaden sky above him and the snow falling soft against his cheeks. The slopes of the draw lay white, and there'd be snow up yonder where the Diamond C gather had been held. Those cattle were long since into the cars and on their way to market. Will breathed deep, liking being outside. He stepped up into the saddle; he thanked Pablo and headed toward the river.

The bay had got fat from Diamond C hay and lazy from inactivity. Will was content to ride slowly. He came past the haystacks and saw Rube Freeman forking out hay to a few cows standing around the wire. He waved to Freeman and soon found himself on the river trail he'd ridden as Littlejohn's prisoner. He came to the vicinity where he'd abandoned Carrico's broken carriage; the carriage had long since been removed. He thought of all that had happened that hectic night and so

271

thought of Buck. Libbie had told him that Buck had been buried on the ridge overlooking B-M's ranch buildings. He knew that Buck was a scar he would wear always. He could tell himself that Buck had given him no choice; he could go over and over the words that had led up to the gun-play, but still there was Buck's smile to remember.

He wondered what new neighbors there'd be at B-M. The ranch's ownership would have to be settled by law, he supposed. According to Littlejohn's letter today, the place hadn't belonged to Millard but to the river-wrecker gang as a syndicate.

He came into Fort Benton in midday. It was no longer snowing, but snow lay on ridge-poles and roofs and powdered the town and capped the high, black bluffs across the river. The cottonwoods stood bare of leaves. He rode along Front Street till he was near the Occidental Saloon. From his saddle, he spoke to a loiterer. "Do you know where I can find a gambler named Carrico?"

The man squinted at him. "If you're in luck you'll catch him at the stage station. Saw him heading that way with his luggage not more than half an hour ago."

"Thanks," Will said.

He rode on to the stage station and dismounted and tied up the bay. Just for an instant the reluctance he'd known at Diamond C a few hours earlier touched him again, and he was tempted to turn away. *Let them go! Let them go!* This was strange, considering how long he'd waited for an answer that might lie beyond the door. He shrugged and went inside.

The heat of a stove blasted to all the corners of a small room; only a few people were here. Carrico and Zoe sat close together on a bench, waiting. He walked directly toward them and saw surprise draw them up stiff and alarm show on them.

He said, "I'm not here to make trouble, Carrico."

Carrico said, "No need. We're getting out, as you can see."

"I owe you for smashing your carriage," Will said. "You can take it out of the wages you never paid me all the years I worked for you."

Carrico said, "That isn't what fetched you."

"No," Will said, "it isn't. I think you know what did. Tell me, Carrico, how much you learned from the orphanage that turned me over to you and your lady."

Carrico said, "Nothing, really. Only that you'd been found adrift in a yawl bearing the name of the *William J. Yeoman.*"

Anger stormed through Will. "You're lying!" he said, but even as he spoke, he knew that Carrico wasn't lying. For Carrico had drawn deep into the collar of his coat and made himself smaller on the bench, and fear had put an ashy tint in Carrico's dark skin. Suddenly Will realized that the real reason why the man was leaving was because he, Will, was in this neighborhood. The proof of this stood in Carrico's eyes. It was queer, Will thought, remembering St. Louis, how things had got turned around so that Carrico was the one who was afraid of him.

Carrico said hastily, "It's the truth. I swear it!"

Will said, "Then I'll go to St. Louis and talk to the sisters at the orphanage."

"You'll get nowhere," Carrico said. "The place burned years ago, and all its records with it." He smiled then; this was the shallow triumph he salvaged.

Will let his hands fall to his sides. He stood now at a blank wall; he had come to a hope's end.

Zoe had been watching him fixedly. She shrugged, her sensuous lips pursed and her eyes scornful. She said, "Why do you have to keep gnawing at this thing? Your folks are likely dead anyway. Will, you're a fool!"

He looked at her, still-faced. All that had ever been between them was dead and had

274

been dead since that moment in her room weeks ago when she'd handed him an unloaded gun and a lie. He wished her no luck and no harm; he wished her nothing. Perhaps he would meet her again, and Carrico, too; he had come to learn that the destinies of people were like tracks in the sand, aimless and yet purposeful, crossing and recrossing. A man turned a corner or took a new fork from an old trail and met yesterday coming toward him. So it would ever be. But next time he would meet these two as strangers.

He turned on his heel and walked out of the stage station, leaving them to each other. They were forever linked, and in that fact would lie the punishment for both. If malice had been his, he could have wished them nothing worse. Instead, he dismissed them from his mind, but he couldn't slough off his deep disappointment. He had counted on what Carrico might have been forced to tell him. Had his reluctance to put the question to Carrico when the chance came been based on some instinct that had whispered there would be no answer?

He led his horse along the street as far as a saloon and went inside and had a drink. He spent a longtime over that drink.

Talk buzzed around him; he learned that the Manitoba track had reached Great Falls and there'd been a big celebration up there. The Manitoba had a new Mogul locomotive running from the Teton siding to the head of Government Coulee. One of the largest, that locomotive, weighing sixty-five tons. He pricked up his ears to talk of recent trouble with the Indians. A company of cavalry and one of infantry had left Fort Keogh for the Cheyenne agency on Tongue River to arrest a Crow named Sword Bearer who had gone with fifty braves to persuade the Cheyennes to join them. Seemed that Sword Bearer was trying to turn back the calendar to another day. Will felt sorry for Sword Bearer and all the ragged, dispossessed ones. Heavy snow and very cold down in that part of Montana where the troops moved. Worse yet over in the Black Hills, where snow blocked travel. Twenty below at St. Paul. In fact, a man said, the St. Paul bartenders were selling whiskey by the square foot.

Will drank. The liquor warmed him, and he liked listening to the hum of talk around him. Here was a town he could tie to, this little place that had come to belong to all the world. Never mind what that man had said in another saloon about Fort Benton's becoming just another cowtown. Like Matt Comfort, Will had his faith in cattle and he would find his future there.

He went outside and climbed onto the bay and took the trail to Diamond C.

Mrs. Comfort was crossing the yard toward the barn as he rode in. He waved to her. Pablo came to the corral and took the reins of the bay and gave Will a wizened Mexican smile. Will walked to the house. He felt very tired and judged that he hadn't yet got all his strength back. Time was what he needed.

He walked in and found Libbie in the living room. This had become a familiar place with its crude furniture, its curtains, its big brass-bound Bible on the table beside Mrs. Comfort's needlework. He took off his hat and unbuttoned Matt Comfort's coat.

Libbie asked, "You saw her?" She put the question with such a lack of interest that her interest stood betrayed.

He nodded. "But it was really Carrico I went to see. You'll mind that I told you about a question I had to ask him. There's no answer to it, Libbie."

She shook her head. "Why was it so very important to you?"

He looked at her. She had come to mean many things to him. She was contentment and the smell of cooking and a soft and comforting footfall. She was the breeze off the river and the good sound of saddle leather creaking on the trail. Once he had decided that she was not a pretty girl; why then had she grown more beautiful to his sight each day? He said, "I've intended to ask you to marry me, Libbie. I wanted to bring you a name that truly belonged to me."

She drew in her breath sharply, and he said, "We could build this place together. We'd both have to work and work hard." For a moment a vision of it all swept before him — the things to be done with land and cattle and buildings, the fruitful, toilsome years stretching ahead. "It won't be easy. You'd have to keep on, just as you've been."

She said, "I think I'd need that, Will. And I know that I need you. I've known it ever since that night by the haystacks when Noonan came riding up and I realized there was at least one job that was a man's job. The trouble's finished. But I've learned a lesson about myself."

"Will the Yeoman name do?" he asked.

She said, "Will, you're a fool," and he started, for those had been Zoe's words. She said, "Have you forgotten the argument of Matt Comfort, the one you told me about, the one that moved you to cross Carrico for my dad's sake? Scrub people have scrub offspring; and when a corner's tight, a man or a steer will show what breed he comes from by the way he acts. All through the trouble, you

278

ran true to breed, Will. That leaves me with no doubt as to what kind of people you came from. I'll be proud to belong to you."

True to breed? He turned her words over in his mind and suddenly he saw that they made sense. More than that, each man made his breed better or worse within his own lifetime. He remembered what Matt Comfort had said on the St. Louis levee: "Each day we live adds up to what makes us what we are." Matt had been speaking of Littlejohn, but it held true for everyone. Buck Harper had come from fine people and so had Carrico, and perhaps Brant Millard, too, but stress had bent them the wrong way. At another forge, Will Yeoman had been hammered out to stand four-square. He was what his bloodline made him, and he was also what the years had made him.

And now he knew why he had felt strangely come home in the bigness of Montana, and why, at the last, he hadn't cared about putting his question to Carrico. Here was a land where the thing that counted was how a man acted, not who his forbears were. Here lay the tolerance of a frontier, and the promise. Here lay a freedom greater than the freedom he'd won from Littlejohn.

He took a step toward Libbie. He asked, "You're sure? You're very sure?"

Her face livened, and she said, "I've known

how you felt about me a long time. You see, you did a lot of talking in your fever after Littlejohn had you sent here. Not till today, when I thought you wanted to see that girl, did I doubt what I meant to you. I'm ashamed of having doubted. I should have remembered what you said in your fever. Oh, Will, are your compliments always roundabout?"

He had no words with which to make reply and no need for them. He drew her to him, and she came willingly. This was the way a man should first meet love, with someone not a stranger and with everything lasting about it, the little goodnesses and the great ones. Here was a fulness of understanding; here were mysteries yet to be explored. This was the way he had dreamed by a hundred campfires that it would be; he had pictured another face, but it was the dream he had really cherished. He felt the warmth of her within his arms, the closeness; and he was content.